THE SEVEN FIRES OF MADEMOISELLE

Carlota is a precocious twelve-year-old who makes elaborate inventions and is devoted to her beautiful, yet eccentric French nanny, Mademoiselle. Despite being courted by all the local eligible bachelors, Mademoiselle never appears interested in men until, at Christmas, Carlota's home-made decorations catch fire, prompting a rushed visit by the fire brigade. Among the tall, athletic firefighters is Nick Kowalski, a short, balding man with whom Mademoiselle falls instantly and passionately in love. She turns to Carlota for help — how can she ever contrive to meet him again and ignite his affections? The answer lies in a box of matches . . .

ESTHER VILAR

THE SEVEN FIRES OF MADEMOISELLE

Complete and Unabridged

ULVERSCROFT
Leicester

First published in Great Britain in 2009 by
Vintage
The Random House Group Limited
London

First Large Print Edition
published 2011
by arrangement with
The Random House Group Limited
London

British Library CIP Data

Vilar, Esther, *1935* –
The seven fires of Mademoiselle.
1. Nannies- -Fiction.
2. Fire fighters- -Washington (D.C.)- -Fiction.
3. Large type books.
I. Title
833.9′14–dc22

ISBN 978–1–44480–702–8

Published by
F. A. Thorpe (Publishing)
Anstey, Leicestershire

Set by Words & Graphics Ltd.
Anstey, Leicestershire
Printed and bound in Great Britain by
T. J. International Ltd., Padstow, Cornwall

This book is printed on acid-free paper

Only four per cent of convicted arsonists are female. Most fires started by women with criminal intention have their origin in suppressed emotions, amongst them most commonly jealousy.

Stephen Barlay
Fire: an international report

'Why don't you come over and play with Caroline some time?'

In everyone's life, there are sentences you don't forget. Not least because the people around you won't let you forget them. In my case it was this sentence that would forever be imprinted on my mind. For the place where it was spoken was Washington DC, the playground mentioned was the White House, the person who uttered it no less a person than John F. Kennedy and the proposed playmate was his little daughter, Caroline.

We are Argentinians and had only moved from Lima to Washington two months earlier, where my father, a diplomat, had been offered a new post at the Argentinian embassy. I had just turned twelve and when the ambassador and his wife invited the children of South American diplomats to their yearly Christmas party there was no way to get out of it. No one had really counted on a personal appearance by Kennedy. They had been prepared for Jackie and the two children, but not the President himself. But suddenly he was announced and a few minutes later he entered the room, without his wife, but hand in hand with his daughter. She was wearing a dark brown satin dress and seemed to be just as enthusiastic about the whole thing as I was.

* * *

I still remember that at that time I was rather unhappy. Like most children of diplomats, I spent much of my childhood moving from one country to the next. As I already mentioned, our previous domicile had been the Peruvian capital, Lima, where I had managed to make real friends with another child for the first time. Her name was Irina and she was one year older than me, a skinny girl with funny pigtails, who read only science fiction stories and was, as far as I was concerned, the most amusing person on earth. And she was precisely the reason why I hated everyone and everything at that time: my parents who had separated us so heartlessly, the large house we occupied here, the elegant people who visited us day in and day out, this town, this country, this reception.

There were about forty of us children dressed up to the nines, who had to stand around a gigantic Christmas tree in the embassy's reception hall. Inside this circle, the President of the United States and his daughter moved from child to child, shaking hands while trying to come up with a few appropriate words to say. Behind each of us stood the adult who had accompanied us to these festivities and who was now trying to prevent the worst. In my case it was my mother, wearing a garment that she had bought just for the occasion and which to me looked like crumpled pyjamas. When I had told her so in the car, she said that our taste in clothes would probably never be the same.

'And who do we have here?' The President's friendly expression was in clear contrast to his daughter's.

'Tell the President your name, darling,' my mother encouraged me, with a voice cooing with tenderness. She was Viennese, but as the offspring of a nouveau riche industrialist family, she had been carted off to English boarding schools as soon as possible and hence her English was completely without accent.

My name? Very well, if they insist: 'Carlitos.'

'Isn't that a boy's name?'

'Yes.' I was nudged in the back and corrected myself: 'Yes, Mr President.'

Of course Carlitos wasn't my real name. It's Carlota. But in the one and a half years I spent with Irina, we had fallen into the habit of changing our first names every few months, forcing everyone to call us by whatever the latest creation was — at least everyone who wanted to get a reaction out of us. Just before they separated us so heartlessly, we had decided on boys' names, which we wouldn't give up as long as they kept us separated. Irina called herself Stanislav, after her favourite writer Stanislav Lem. I acquired, far less imaginatively, the name Carlitos. It was a pity that my friend couldn't witness that even here, confronted by the most powerful man in the world, I was sticking to our agreement.

'You have amazing pigtails, Carlitos. Who plaited them for you? Your mother?' My mother and plaiting! What a joke! She hated this hairstyle, and as I am a blonde as well, had even gone as far as telling me that it made me look like the child of a Nazi. But it was an exact copy of my faraway girlfriend's hair and a further manifestation of my protest. Every time they looked at me, my parents should be reminded of their cruelty.

Before my mother could nudge me for a second time, I decided on a reluctant murmur: 'Mademoiselle.'

'I can't hear you, son.' The President leaned down to me with such a broad smile that I could have counted his shiny white teeth, that is if I had wanted to.

'Mademoiselle does it for me!'

'Our nanny, Mr President,' hurried my mother. 'She comes from France.'

'Then one can only hope she likes it here.' The remark was clearly directed at me. After all, this was a children's party.

That was my big opportunity and I shouted: 'No, she doesn't like it here, and nor do I!'

The silence was brief, but absolute. The small Mexican boy next to me turned and looked at me, his eyes wide open.

'Well, maybe you haven't made the right friends yet?' Kennedy said. And then came that historic sentence: 'Why don't you come over and play with Caroline some time?'

'What a wonderful idea, Mr President!' I had rarely heard my mother's voice so excited. 'I really think she is a little lonely!' I exchanged a short glance with the girl named Caroline, whose expression had turned from one of boredom into open disgust. How old could she be? Not older than seven. Couldn't her father see that I was a whole head taller than her? But before I could protest, he had moved on to the Mexican boy.

* * *

When we were finally sitting in the car, against all my expectations, my mother wasn't angry at all. She brought the sentence home with her and passed it on to my ecstatic father, who from then on would repeat it to everyone who came to visit us. And of course there were no more complaints about my hairstyle.

Introductions now went something like this: 'And this is Carlota, our daughter. Carlota, come here and shake the senator's hand.'

'What a beautiful little girl! And what delightful pigtails!'

'Indeed. Even your President has a weakness for them. As soon as he set eyes on her, he invited her to the White House to play with his little daughter.' At this point he tended to turn to me, as if he couldn't remember her name: 'Caroline, isn't it?'

Eleven months later, after Kennedy's assassination, it became even worse: 'Kennedy? But of course we knew him personally. Our daughters had started a big little friendship with each other. Caroline, poor child!' Complete nonsense, of course, as neither then nor later did I ever play with Caroline.

I hardly noticed the tragedy in Dallas. For

only a few days after this reception, December 24th to be precise, my life was freed from all gloom overnight. To this day I think that the months between Christmas '62 and the day Lee Harvey Oswald fired his fatal shots were the most exhilarating of my life.

For on Christmas Eve 1962, at around eight o'clock, Catherine Loucheron, our gorgeous French nanny, whom we never called anything but Mademoiselle, started the first of her fires. And amongst the men in the approaching fire engine was Nick Kowalski, a fireman of Washington DC's fire department.

In those days, my parents liked to consider themselves politically on the Left, at least in private circles. But as much as I tried, I couldn't find any practical evidence for this. The ivy-covered brown-stone house in the fashionable district of Georgetown that we moved into — not three hundred metres from the one where the Kennedys used to live before their move into the White House — was certainly one of the most modest in my long chain of childhood domiciles. But as far as I can recall, it still sported a good dozen rooms, a basement apartment for the servants, two garages and a small garden, overgrown with bamboo. At the end of the garden was a swimming pool, complete with a little house for changing in. If my father ever shared his diplomat's salary with some needy people, I hadn't heard anything about it.

This leftist label was also hardly appropriate considering our origins. My Argentinian grandparents were living in a villa in Buenos Aires that was so large that I regularly got lost in it when I was very little. When one summer holiday I planned to walk around their estate in one of the northern provinces, I was informed that this endeavour would take the best part of two weeks. My mother's family on the other hand gave the appearance of being more modest, but that presumably had more to do with European sensitivity than matters of wealth. My Viennese grandmother's long-distance calls were feared, as once she got started it usually took a hundred years before she would replace the receiver.

'What does 'left' actually mean?' I once asked my father.

'When you're on the side of the weak.'

'So you give them your money?'

'That would be more like charity. A true left-winger will treat every person as an equal amongst equals. For example, being left can also mean that one is nice to one's servants.'

* * *

That must have also been why it was the most natural thing in the world for Mademoiselle to eat dinner with us, at least for the first weeks after her arrival. Not only on those rare occasions when we were dining alone, but also when we entertained guests, no matter how high-ranking they were. Anyway, she wasn't a normal kind of nanny: she came from Biarritz, where her father ran a successful nightclub, and she had passed the French baccalaureate, known as one of the most difficult examinations in the world. And she was not exactly employed to take care of me — when Georgetown Day School's yellow school bus dropped me back home it was already four o'clock in the afternoon — but to teach me as much of her exquisite French in my free time as possible. As my father had his eye on the French embassy, my parents had insisted that a cassette accompanied all applications for the post of nanny. When the time came, their beloved daughter must not have been allowed to fall into a linguistic vacuum.

* * *

However, it soon transpired that God wasn't very good at thanking my parents for their penchant for social equality. Of course we had already recognised Mademoiselle's enormous beauty when we picked her up from Washington's airport and first saw her coming through customs. Despite the fact that she was wearing a rather boring woollen jumper and had neatly knotted her magnificent hair behind her neck, my father, drilled at diplomats' school in the art of casual conversation, was at a loss for words. 'The face of a Madonna and the body of a whore,' I once heard him describe her to a friend on the telephone. 'No, not in a million years,' he added — presumably replying to an enquiry about whether the caller would have a chance with her. 'Forget everything you've heard about French women, pal. This one's made of stone.'

Not even my usually so instinctive mother was able to foresee what effect Mademoiselle's looks would have on her dinner parties. Every good hostess likes to have attractive women at her table, as she knows that they will stimulate the other guests. And not only the male ones, as, according to one of my Viennese grandmother's bons mots, men and women basically have only one interest in common: women. But Catherine Loucheron's beauty was too spectacular to be of service to my mother's ambitions as a hostess.

It soon transpired that her presence made any normal dinner conversation impossible. As much as you tried to exude an air of disinterest, you simply had to look at her.

* * *

Not even I, the child, was immune to Mademoiselle's spell, even though today, three decades later, I can't really put my finger on where it originated. It was probably the combination of many things. Her magnificent pebble-grey eyes which, due to a slight squint, always looked a little surprised — as if whoever she turned to had just said something unbelievably exciting. Her thick dark-blonde hair, which she usually carelessly tied in a knot so that a few strands would always fall across her high cheekbones. Her — at least according to conventional standards of beauty — much too large mouth with the always unmadeup voluptuous lips which, when she was laughing, revealed absolutely perfect white teeth. Even though back then I had nothing to compare it with, her figure must also have been quite impressive. To this day, I can hear the enthusiastic whistles of the workers at a building site on N Street, which we passed on the way to my piano lessons.

On top of all that, the Americans must have been smitten by her French accent, as they never tired of asking her questions, no matter how superfluous:

'You grew up by the sea, mademoiselle? You must be a good swimmer?'

'Yes, I am, monsieur.'

'Would you agree that the French cuisine is the best in the world?'

'I don't know. I've never really travelled much.'

'But where did you learn to speak English?'

'Our nanny taught me. She was English.'

A nanny with a nanny, would you believe it? However, as my parents' friends also pretended to be broad-minded, no one wondered about that out loud.

* * *

As Mademoiselle must have been aware of her special situation — presumably she had experienced nothing else since puberty and I can imagine that even at kindergarten she attracted more attention than the other children — she spoke as little as possible. But as she was hired, amongst other things, to supervise my table manners, as soon as she uttered the slightest criticism any conversation would come to an immediate halt. No one wanted to miss out on the tone of her voice, the elegant line her neck made when she leaned over to me, the movements of her delicate hands when she showed me how to deal with a lobster claw. Should her serviette fall to the floor in the course of this, everyone rushed to help her so she wouldn't have to bend down. If she asked for one of the salt cellars, arms extended from everywhere. The smile she acknowledged it with was obviously more interesting than any political controversy which one had concerned oneself with just moments earlier. Male guests especially tended to deliver endless monologues, as they hoped that this would be the quickest way to impress her. If someone knew a snippet of French, he'd repeat it again and again: *'N'est-ce pas, mademoiselle?'* And when at the end of the meal she leaned back to smoke one of her Gauloises Bleu, everyone wanted to be the one to light it for her.

* * *

When someone handed my mother a newspaper clipping during an especially important dinner, and she asked Mademoiselle to fetch her reading glasses which she had left in the library, it was, as they say, the straw that broke the camel's back. Immediately three men jumped up to spare the beautiful nanny the trouble, and my parents' remaining love for equality evaporated in an instant. An excuse was found quickly. After all, the child was still at school at lunch, and as far as dinner was concerned my mother found the ingenious solution of moving my bedtime forward. The child looks tired, the child needs more sleep. From that point on, Mademoiselle and I were eating on our own, an hour before everyone else, in the small breakfast room next to the kitchen. Only at weekends, when there was no school the following day, were we still allowed at the formal dinner table. But then my parents usually went out anyway.

As the idea about my going to bed early was quickly forgotten, the new regulations suited 'the child' down to the ground. At last I wouldn't have to bear any more boring dinner conversations and was no longer disturbed in my thoughts with an 'And what does our little Carlota make of the new amendment?' My thoughts generally concerned epoch-making inventions. Besides I was unbelievably proud to finally have the much-coveted Mademoiselle all to myself. Our conversations were quite amusing, at least as long as she didn't insist on speaking

French with me. And in contrast to the other grown-ups, she would even let me talk to her about my inventions.

Unfortunately, it quickly transpired that I couldn't talk to her about the other two subjects that interested me most at that time: sex and religion. I have to admit that to this day I haven't found topics of conversation that fascinate me as much as they do. Sex concerns the art of enjoying nature's preprogrammed, people-making instinct without actually making any. Religion concerns the art of circumventing nature's pre-programmed death by believing in some form of continuation. In the end, sex stands for life, and religion for death. What could be more interesting, even if only as a topic of conversation?

But Mademoiselle was a Catholic, and that must have meant that the pleasure of sex without making humans wasn't allowed to her, while an afterlife in paradise was guaranteed, even in writing. So why should she get worked up about my favourite subjects? Just my bad luck.

* * *

Of course we didn't talk about our banishment to the breakfast room either. But the reason was perfectly clear, even to a twelve-year-old: Mademoiselle would never be an equal amongst equals — her beauty not only set her apart from the poor, but also from the rich. In this case, it wasn't just my parents who lacked social justice, but the Creator himself, as evidently He had created this spectacular 'class enemy'. You can give away your money, but how can you share your beauty with the underprivileged? Should Mademoiselle have disfigured herself in order to be more like the other women at my parents' dinner table?

Even though I was at an age at which you begin mercilessly to expose even the slightest grown-ups' character weaknesses, I didn't for a moment think of my mother's actions as revenge against an underling who happened to be more attractive than the lady of the house. At least then, in the months before the disaster, my mother seemed to admire Mademoiselle just as much as I did. More often than not, she'd return from her shopping trips with a garment for Mademoiselle she thought she would look good in. And of course she was right: after all Mademoiselle looked good in everything.

What I could only suspect back then I now know from my own experience: there is a degree of female perfection that silences any kind of jealousy in other women. Rather you get the urge to carry a banner in front of a perfect example of your own sex: Look here, you men, this is how beautiful we can be! By the way, my mother was also an attractive woman. But no one was as attractive as Mademoiselle.

* * *

Of course Mademoiselle was in no way hurt by the 'demotion'. It must have been a relief for her to get rid of her admirers so easily. The clusters of men staring at her when we were shopping on M Street were already more than enough. Whenever we went for walks in Georgetown — as a European she apparently found it hard to do without her daily walk — it seemed as if all the district's male inhabitants were constantly getting lost, so often were we asked the way — usually through a car window. Occasionally we amused ourselves by sending the admirer in the opposite direction. Even though he of course knew the right way, he was then forced to head off — after many thank-yous and a last glance at my spectacular nanny — in the wrong direction.

'*Pauvre idiot*,' Mademoiselle would then say, laughing. Yet she laughed without gloating, as beautiful people usually are kinder than the rest of us. As the indifference we show towards the unprepossessing deeply scars their psyche, they are more likely to resort to tricks or lies to get our attention than those we already take notice of — like Mademoiselle. So the beautiful amongst us can allow themselves the luxury of a straightforward and pleasant character. Apart from the way she treated the New Age hairdresser — I'll tell you more about her later — I've never seen Mademoiselle being mean to anyone.

* * *

Even though now she was more or less safe from pursuers in our house, there were still some persistent ones on her heels, remainders from the weeks of the shared joys at the dining table. I can especially recall a red-haired lawyer called Christopher, one of Kennedy's former election assistants and at that time a consultant on his brother the Attorney General's staff. In my father's opinion he was one of Washington's up-and-coming politicians. There was also a newly appointed ambassador — I can no longer remember from which Scandinavian country — who was tireless in his efforts. Being a good friend, he was championed by my father as far as the race to get Mademoiselle's attention was concerned.

'And you don't like him at all?' I once heard him ask her after he left.

'*Mais si, il est sympa.*' Yet you could not read more than politeness into her reply.

Then Mademoiselle evidently conquered the heart of a young, fantastically handsome star surgeon at Georgetown University Hospital. As he lived close by, we once had called him for help when the visiting Argentinian trade minister became unwell. Mademoiselle did nothing more than open the door for him and lead him to the patient. He returned the next day, in a brand-new BMW, and invited her for a drive.

But after this excursion, she wouldn't even take his phone calls and, without a word, gave the bunches of flowers he sent to our cook. The poor guy tried to enlist my father as a go-between, arranging to play golf with him as often as possible. Yet whenever he came back to our house for a drink afterwards, Mademoiselle left through the back door. Soon you could hear her favourite French singers — Brel, Brassens, Aznavour — from the basement apartment, which she occupied on her own as the other employees went home at night. I think those first few weeks in Washington she suffered as much from homesickness as I did from longing for my distant friend.

* * *

'She shouldn't be so choosy,' my father once said to my mother. 'Beauty doesn't last forever, even she should know that.'

'But maybe she isn't looking for a man?'

'Nonsense. She doesn't play nanny in Washington for nothing. This is the control centre of the universe. You can meet the most powerful men in the world. I think she's craftier than you think.' You couldn't miss the hurt tone in his voice. It can't have been easy for my father to be so blatantly ignored.

'Then maybe she's waiting for a prince?' my mother said, used to trouble in this department. She picked up the new *Vogue* and was looking for her reading glasses, as usual.

'I bet that no one below a Kennedy will do for her.'

However, Mademoiselle was neither waiting for a prince, nor a Kennedy. She was waiting for someone like Nick Kowalski.

* * *

About two weeks before he entered Mademoiselle's, or, to be more precise, our lives, we were both sitting at our solitary dinner table. When Franca, the Italian cook, was out of earshot I asked Mademoiselle: 'Did you come to America to find a husband?'

She looked at me, her pebble-grey eyes even more surprised than usual: 'Who said that?'

'My father.'

'*Le vieil idiot!*' She actually sounded angry. Probably he was chasing her a little too vehemently with his unrestrainable self-confidence — who could take on an Argentinian?

'But is it true?'

She thought about it and then also unfortunately remembered her duty to talk to me in French: '*Qu'est-ce que tu veux entendre, Charlotte? La vérité ou un petit mensonge?*'

'The truth.'

'*Eh bien: oui.*'

'Yes?'

'Yes, I came here to look for a man. A man to marry, *voilà*.'

'To marry!' I pretended to throw up. 'I'll never get married. And neither will Stanislav.'

'*Et qui est* Stanislav?'

When she saw my deeply disappointed expression she hit her forehead. 'Stanislav, *mais oui!* But you say that now. I'll be twenty-five next month and, believe me, it's not good when a woman is on her own.'

'I'm going to become an inventor,' I said. 'Inventors like being alone because they need time to think.'

'Perhaps. But I am nothing and don't want to become anything. All I want is a man and lots of children. *Voilà*.'

'So why don't you pick one? Franca says you could have anyone you wanted. What about this ridiculous lawyer? Franca says that one day he might be president.'

'*C'est bien possible*.'

'The surgeon with his stupid BMW? Everyone is after him.'

'Says Franca.'

'Says my mother.'

She laughed. '*Un connaisseur de vins*.'

'What does that mean?'

'A wine connoisseur.'

'And what's wrong with a man who knows about wines?'

'It's provincial. Now eat.'

'And the ambassador?' I asked.

'An imbecile.'

'How do you know?'

'Because no one with any sense would become ambassador,' she said. 'And now it's time to eat!'

'And what would someone have to be to please you?'

The answer came without hesitation. 'He'd have to be a man.'

'And the surgeon isn't one?'

'Not a real one.'

'Then what is a real man?'

'I have no idea. But I'll know as soon as I meet one. Then I'll let you know, *d'accord?*'

When we had finished our food, she leant back and, as always, lit one of the Gauloises her sister Danielle sent her from France. Every month a parcel with two cartons of Gauloises Bleu and ten boxes of French matches would arrive. I never saw her use a lighter.

* * *

With Christmas around the corner, Mademoiselle's homesickness became visibly worse. Yet there had already been a lot of snow that year in Washington. Snow-covered Georgetown looked like a small town out of an American musical and our Japanese gardener, Mr Fudimoto, would arrive at the break of day by bus from the opposite side of town to clear away the snow in front of our varnished garage doors. And in a way our house was like one out of a fairy tale. Before we moved in, it had been painted sky blue while the front door, the window shutters and the two garage doors were varnished in black. The front door was adorned with golden handles, and an old-fashioned gas lantern — not a rarity in this district — stood next to the steps that led up to it. Mr Fudimoto had to light it every evening. And of course snow made everything look twice as homely.

But the snow didn't make Mademoiselle feel better: she informed me that it doesn't snow in Biarritz around Christmas. When I came home from school, we wandered over to the letterbox on Wisconsin Avenue, where she deposited the mountains of Christmas cards she had written that morning.

'You have so many friends?' I asked her, impressed.

'Why not?'

'Any men?'

'Only girlfriends,' she informed me. 'A woman can't be friends with a man. At least not with someone from the same generation. Either she likes him, then she likes him completely — also as a man — and then it becomes love. Or she doesn't like him and then there can also be no friendship. Why should a woman become friends with a man she doesn't like?'

'And a homosexual?'

'Where did you get that word from?'

I had heard it from my mother, of course.

She always explained everything I wanted to know. I never had to be told 'the facts of life' as nothing was ever kept from me. 'Can't a woman become friends with a homosexual?'

Mademoiselle thought about it. 'In that case it must be different.'

* * *

However, what she missed most was her family. She was the oldest of seven siblings and had left behind five sisters and a two-year-old brother in Biarritz. Judging by her stories, her home seems to have been a happy one. Her mother had been a stripper in her father's establishment, but only for one night.

'Only for one night?'

'When a man really loves a woman, he wouldn't like seeing her parading naked in front of other men, would he?'

'Not even in France?'

'*Surtout pas en France*. Maybe in Paris, but Biarritz? Never!'

It really seemed to be a happy family. At least everyone was laughing in the one photo she showed me. Her little brother was holding his little socks in his hand and stretching his naked legs up in the air. It was impossible to overlook the resemblance between Mademoiselle and her mother.

✽

Our tree was delivered four days before Christmas. It wasn't as gigantic as the one in the ambassador's villa, but still so big that Mr Fudimoto had to cut it down before he could put it up in the library. Even then Leonard, my father's driver, had to help him. Our Christmas tree decorations hadn't arrived in time along with some other things from Lima, and as I didn't stop begging, I was finally put in charge of decorating the magnificent tree. Under Mademoiselle's supervision, it goes without saying.

As it turned out, she neither liked traditional Christmas decorations nor the silver lametta that was the custom in my grandmother's Austrian home. Its arrangement and removal would keep us busy for hours every year. She didn't even want to know about my beloved glass balls.

'What's wrong with glass balls?'

'*Trop vulgaires*.'

'What would you hang on a Christmas tree?'

'*Rien de tout*. Nothing at all. An undecorated pine tree with a few candles.

There isn't anything more beautiful, is there?'

But this time it was my turn to disagree: where would that leave me and my mission? So we agreed on handmade Christmas decorations: cookies, which you could take off the tree and eat, as next year the family's decorations would again be at our disposal. But no angels, no stars and no Father Christmases, Mademoiselle insisted. They would have to be imaginative. 'Art to eat,' she said, '*de l'art à manger*.' (Maybe she anticipated the 'eat art' movement.)

The results of our combined efforts were astonishing. Especially Franca, the cook from Bologna, who Mademoiselle insisted looked like Pope John XXIII, developed hitherto unknown talents. In those pre-Christmas days, she invented the first edible American flag amongst many other things. Stars and Stripes in the brightest sugar colours, a Jasper Johns of confectionery.

All that was missing were the candles. While we could find countless varieties of electric candles on our expeditions through the stores in the surrounding area, wax candles and the holders to attach them to the branches were nowhere to be seen. The white-haired owner of a general store finally enlightened us. In the United States the use of wax candles on Christmas trees was forbidden.

'Do you know how many millions of dollars' damage are caused by fires every year?'

'Dollars, dollars,' Mademoiselle said impatiently. 'I come from Europe, monsieur. For me a Christmas tree with electric candles is not a Christmas tree.'

'And your firemen? Are they happy when every Christmas they have to jump into the ovens of your burning houses like stuffed turkeys?'

I chuckled appreciatively: I couldn't have put it better myself. And I preferred electric candles anyway. Especially those that went on and off, like the ones in American movies. We had never had any of those before!

But Mademoiselle wouldn't budge. 'So you won't sell me any candles?'

'I'm not allowed to. It's illegal.'

'But when all the lights go off in a house . . . ' She turned to me. 'What is it called?'

'A short circuit.'

'But then you need candles, surely?'

'But that's different.'

She smiled her bewitching smile. 'Then sell me candles just in case there's a short circuit in our house at Christmas.'

The storeowner sighed, but after all he also was a man. 'Very well, how many do you need?'

'Three dozen.'

'That's too many!'

'Two dozen. But red ones!'

On our way home, she suddenly stopped dead in her tracks. '*Qu'est-ce que je suis idiote!* Do you know why he sold us the candles? Because we can't put them on the tree! They can't stop selling wax candles at Christmas time, but we won't get candle holders anywhere!'

'No problem.'

'No problem? We have a dark tree!'

'There's some wire and tools in the basement. I'll invent some candle holders!'

'You can do that?'

'Sure.'

She embraced me right there and then. 'Carlitos, you're a genius.'

⋆ ⋆ ⋆

So that's how the first fire started. The edible sculptures were dangling gracefully from the branches, the candles stood straight in my handmade wire spirals, the wrapped presents were decoratively distributed around the tree and the German Christmas songs my mother loved so much sounded out from the gramophone. Mademoiselle used her French matches to festively light 'her' candles, and then we opened both wings of the large door and asked my parents, who were waiting in the drawing room, to enter for the giving out of presents.

Our Christmas tree was a great success. My mother never tired of praising each and every one of our artistic efforts and thought that our decorations were much too beautiful to be eaten. When all the presents were finally unwrapped and the real as well as the faked cries of delight had died away (my parents had managed to track down a complete collection of Edith Piaf's recordings for Mademoiselle), we all went to the dining room, which was located on the other side of the ground floor. In line with their social convictions, my parents had given all the employees the day off. Mademoiselle and I took over the warming up and serving of the prepared Christmas dinner.

We were still eating the starter when my father observed that there was a burning smell. Mademoiselle hurried, napkin in her hand, to the kitchen as she thought something had gone wrong with the Christmas roast, but returned almost instantly. '*C'est l'arbre! C'est l'arbre!*' she screamed. 'It's the tree!'

We threw back our chairs and rushed into the library. At first we could see nothing due to the large amount of smoke, but then we could clearly make out flames at the bottom of the tree. It would only be a matter of seconds before they would engulf it all.

* * *

And now everyone started to panic in his or her own way. My mother ran out into the snow-covered street dressed in her low-cut evening dress, from where I could hear her scream 'Fire! Fire!' In German! My father pulled a bunch of books off the shelves and started to concern himself with rescuing the documents and valuables from his hidden safe. But in the panic, he couldn't remember the combination, and turned the dial, coughing and swearing.

As if there were no other telephones in the house, Mademoiselle leapt to the receiver in the library and asked us, fanning the air with her handkerchief as if she could disperse the smoke, for the number of the fire department. But none of us had been in the country long enough to know it. At least my father could remember the number of the international operator. They immediately offered to call the fire department. Mademoiselle spelt out our address through the napkin and then promptly let herself fall into one of the leather armchairs.

As I was told later again and again I, the child, was the only one who stayed calm. From my expeditions through the house I knew that a rolled-up garden hose was hanging near the stairs to the basement. I dragged it to the toilet situated next to the library, attached it to the golden tap of the washbasin, unrolled it through the increasingly thick smoke, and pointed the surprisingly strong water jet at the burning tree. It didn't take more than a minute or two to extinguish the fire completely.

I turned to the adults standing behind me. 'That's it.'

In the meantime, attracted by my mother's screams, a few festively dressed neighbours had appeared and shuffled over the soaked carpet, laughing and coughing, to embrace me. Only Mademoiselle remained in her armchair like a statue. '*C'était ma faute*,' she mumbled again and again. 'That was all my fault!'

Finally it occurred to someone that we should cancel the fire department. But of course they were already on their way, and a few seconds later they turned into Olive Street, their sirens howling.

* * *

We all ran out into the street, all apart from Mademoiselle. The remaining neighbours who hadn't been at our house now also emerged, so that eventually more or less all the inhabitants of Olive Street were assembled. The Pakistani ambassador, who was living in the corner house, had appeared in his turban.

It was only nine o'clock in the evening, but as it was already dark the appearance of the fire engines with their sirens and flashing lights was even more impressive than it would have been during daylight. There were two fire engines. Two men were sitting in the first, which only consisted of a driver's cab and a gigantic water tank. The second fire engine was at least three times as long, as it had to accommodate the ladder. With it arrived five firemen — two sitting in the driver's cab, two on the outside directly behind it, and in some sort of hut at the end of the fire engine sat the fifth one. And all of them were in full uniform — the yellow fireproof jackets, the helmets, the high boots — just like the fire department you know from action movies. And all that because of a burning Christmas tree.

My father and I ran towards them making wild gestures, which were meant to signify that the danger was averted. Even so they only switched off the sirens when they had finally stopped in front of our house. Then they got out, all cool as cucumbers.

My father introduced himself — quickly mentioning his diplomat's status, probably to be on the safe side — and told them what had happened. One of the firemen then returned to the first fire engine and used the radio to recall the other fire engines also on the way.

As it was icy cold, the neighbours soon began to disappear back into their houses. The firemen had assembled on the sidewalk and were chatting to each other as if the whole matter didn't concern them in the slightest. A few of them had taken off their helmets and started to light cigarettes. Others tried to keep themselves warm by rubbing themselves and hopping around. Most of them didn't seem much older than thirty. Five of them were black and so tall that you could have jumped to the conclusion that height was the decisive factor as far as gaining employment in the American fire department was concerned. One of those who had taken off his helmet was white, also very tall and with blond hair which reached down to his collar. Then there was one of medium height, whom everyone addressed as Chief.

This one now ordered the driver of the fire engine which was carrying the ladder to turn back to the fire station. He then asked my father to take him to the location of the fire. He said that firstly he would have to make sure that the fire was well and truly extinguished, and could no longer flare up. Secondly he would have to write a report, not least because of the insurance company. It was Nick Kowalski.

* * *

That's how he came to enter our house to start the examination of the scene of the fire, without once looking at Mademoiselle, who was still cowering in the armchair. He expressed his regret to my mother about the ruined carpet and asked who had had the idea of the garden hose.

'That was our daughter,' my father said and pushed me towards the expert as living proof.

'Well done, young lady,' he said and patted me on the back.

'May I ask how long you've been in our country?' The question was directed at my father.

'Since October.'

'Then of course you couldn't have known that it is illegal to use Christmas candles made of wax in the United States.'

'I really didn't know that.'

And now Mademoiselle finally awoke from her trance. 'Even if he had known, monsieur, the only person to blame for this fire is me!'

Nick Kowalski, who at that precise moment was busy examining the wet, charred branches, turned to her. In contrast to all the other men who first met her, he mustered a friendly, yet by no means excessively interested glance. Yet Mademoiselle had rarely looked as ravishing as on that Christmas Eve. The black cocktail dress which my mother had recently brought back for her from New York left her shoulders bare and gave her, in addition to her beauty, a touch of vulnerability.

'And who are you?'

'Mademoiselle Loucheron is engaged as our nanny,' my father explained. 'She is French and moved to the United States only two weeks after our arrival.'

'With Air France,' I said in a vain attempt to change the subject.

'Yes, but it was me who decorated this Christmas tree,' Mademoiselle said.

'With my help!' I yelled out.

'Yes, but I lit the candles.'

'And of course you didn't know about the law against their use?'

There wasn't the slightest hint of hesitation in Mademoiselle's voice. 'No, monsieur.'

‘Who sold you the candles?’ Kowalski asked. I noticed that he smiled while asking his questions. But it wasn’t the kind of smile which encouraged getting closer, just the opposite — it kept you at a distance. Furthermore he spoke with an accent which I found hard to pin down. My friend Stanislav spoke that way whenever she pretended to be a Martian.

‘I found them here in the house. In every house there are candles in case of a short circuit.’

Nick Kowalski estimated the number of candles on the tree, squinting his eyes. ‘There must’ve been at least twenty.’

‘I suppose in a household like this everything is in abundance,’ Mademoiselle sighed.

‘And that?’ He had taken one of my candle holders from the tree.

‘I made the holders myself. I’m quite talented in these kinds of things.’

‘Of course had you tried to buy them, you would have found out that it is illegal to use Christmas candles made out of wax, and logically you would have kept well away from it.’

‘Naturally, monsieur.’

Kowalski was leaning over one of the branches and recovered a small, charred object. He held it up to her. 'Miss, I'm sorry to tell you that one of your handmade masterpieces caused this fire. This so-called candle holder obviously turned over with the candle, which lit the branch below.' His voice became stricter: 'Unfortunately it is my duty to inform you that, according to the laws of our country, you can expect a judicial inquiry and, in certain circumstances, may even be charged with negligent arson.'

I could no longer remain quiet. 'The candle holders . . . '

Mademoiselle interrupted. 'Charlotte, *je t'en prie!*' She turned to Nick Kowalski. 'That is no more than just, monsieur. That is also the way one would handle this matter in France.'

There it was again, that smile. 'That's a relief.' His voice clearly sounded ironic. I had never heard a man speak to her in that way. 'Of course it may well be that this matter is not taken further. After all, you have only just arrived in this country. I'll write my report and then we shall see.'

'So then I wait to hear from you, monsieur?'

The reply came as a short, dry laugh. 'Not from me, Miss. I'm only a fireman.'

'But in case it doesn't go any further, then you will let me know?'

Kowalski took a bemused look at the beauty in the shoulder-free evening dress. 'You will be kept informed.'

'Yes, monsieur.' Mademoiselle pretended to be obsequiously happy. When he wanted to turn away from her, she asked: 'Chief?'

'Yes?'

'I would like to thank you.'

He pointed his thumb in my direction. 'It's her you have to thank.'

Nonetheless, Mademoiselle looked up at him with her most delightful smile. Yet Nick Kowalski took his notepad out of his pocket, uninterestedly, and started to take notes for his report.

* * *

Despite the holidays, which only now really began for Americans, the cleaning-up operation started the next day. Mr Fudimoto brought his two sons along with him, and they carried all the books from the landlord's extensive library, along with all other pieces of furniture, into the basement. The furniture in the living room also had to be removed, as my generous watering had ruined the egg-white carpet there too. My mother suggested we fly to Europe to spend Christmas in her parents' chalet in Altaussee, a village in the Steiermark, which she had loved in her childhood. Apparently Sigmund Freud used to spend his summers there. However, the rest of us didn't really feel up to it.

I didn't know whether it was due to Mademoiselle's bad conscience that during the days after the fire I hardly saw her. Certainly it was also my fault. The mishap had stirred my ambition: I wanted to come up with an invention that would bring back the joy of Christmas celebration to the inhabitants of my host country by allowing them to celebrate it with real candles! My concept was of deceptive simplicity: glass balls to hang on Christmas trees. From the outside they would look like ordinary glass balls, however they would be a little larger and also a little more robust. As they would be filled with a mixture of water and carbonic acid, they would have to be able to carry some weight. If an unsupervised Christmas tree caught fire, as had happened to ours, the sphere above the heat source would first get warmer, then heat up, then burst and consequently the extinguishing fluid would pour over the source of the fire and suffocate it before it had a chance to spread.

It was because of this invention that I avoided Mademoiselle after this first fire.

Usually she managed to make me confess any sort of secret with her quietly amazed look. Which reminds me that I forgot to mention another particularity of her eyes. In the upper half of her right iris was a tiny dark brown dot. An optician in Biarritz had told her that this would become larger and larger over the years, so that towards the end of her life she would have two different-coloured eyes, one grey and one brown. Since I heard about it, I always found myself checking whether the dot had become any larger since our previous meeting.

Mademoiselle would be the first to see the plans once they were completed. In contrast to my mother she had real interest in my ideas. I was sure she'd be just as relieved and excited as I was.

* * *

I was able to keep my secret until the 31st of December. I spent my free hours in the much too lavishly equipped basement workshop, where I was experimenting on the optimal mixture of water and carbonic acid. But then came New Year's Eve. My parents had been invited by someone of the scale of the Harrimans or the Kissingers and, feeling concerned, asked me whether I wouldn't be sad to be left alone with Mademoiselle. On the one hand they found it unbelievable that someone like her didn't have a date for such an occasion, but on the other they gladly accepted her offer to keep me company. There was a bottle of champagne ready for her in the refrigerator, with the express permission that I too could drink from it, 'but only a small glass'. When they were leaving, they laughed mischievously, reminding us that we shouldn't set the house on fire again. Farewell words they would use on many occasions — at least until they turned all too poignant and never passed their lips again. But by then Mademoiselle was no longer with us.

Mademoiselle was unusually quiet that New Year's Eve. Homesickness, I thought. At midnight we put on our winter coats and walked out into the deserted street lined with snow-covered maple and magnolia trees. New Year's Eve in a place like Georgetown was a strange affair. As its inhabitants were thrown together from all imaginable countries, a midnight walk was like a walk around a child's globe. In one house they awaited the coming of the New Year in absolute silence, in the next they ignored it completely as they were observing another calendar, in the third they started to throw old furniture out onto the street precisely at midnight — a chair thrown out from the second-floor window of some Italian's villa almost hit us — in the next house they were throwing glasses. Then there were families who celebrated with jumping jacks and firing salutes, others still brought in the New Year with fireworks.

Having returned from our expedition, we opened the champagne. For me it was the first serious experience of alcohol and it was characteristic. As soon as we had clinked glasses and said our toast — I to France, she to Argentina — and I had two or three sips, I began to tell her about my invention. Even though not all the problems had yet been solved — not even the diameter of the balls had been determined — I couldn't help talking to her about it. And in all possible detail. But Mademoiselle didn't say a thing.

'Don't you understand?' I asked impatiently. 'Our accident at Christmas, that's ancient history! Berlin, Vienna, New York, Buenos Aires — everywhere people can celebrate with real candles from now on! Because of my invention, the lighting of candles on a Christmas tree will be as harmless as switching on a hairdryer!'

I stopped, exhausted, and looked at her full of expectation. Was she struck dumb or something?

‘And what about the fire department?’ she finally asked.

‘They can celebrate too. With their own Christmas trees and real candles!’

Mademoiselle suddenly began to laugh loudly. I glanced at the bottle: while I was telling her about my invention she had finished most of it.

‘Are you drunk?’

‘Maybe, Carlitos, maybe! And I have been for days!’

‘And what do you think?’

‘About what?’

‘About my invention!’

‘*Que ce serait dommage*.’ She poured herself another glass and also filled mine.

‘What would be a pity?’

‘If everyone had your invention. Then they would be superfluous, firemen.’ This laugh again.

My patience was beginning to run out. I had never revealed one of my secrets so cheaply. ‘You’re drunk!’

She put down her glass, and took my hand, smiling. ‘Carlitos . . . I promised you that I’d tell you.’

I withdrew my hand. ‘Tell me what?’

‘When I meet him. The man. The one I want to marry. *Eh bien: il est arrivé!*’

I turned around instinctively.

She laughed. 'Not here, silly! But he came. A few days ago.'

'Came where?'

'Here. Into our home. Into your home, your parents' home.'

'Did I meet him?'

'Of course you did. Think about it!'

I tried to recollect the men who had visited us over the past few days. Apart from the surgeon, who had delivered a tiny Christmas tree for her, I couldn't think of anyone.

'The surgeon,' I said. 'I thought so!'

'*Est-ce que tu es folle?*'

'But there was no one else here. At least not someone your age.'

'Think back. Think back to Christmas.'

'Santa Claus!' Now it was I who had to laugh.

'Don't be silly. What happened at Christmas?'

'We made the newspapers,' I giggled.

'There you are, there was a fire. And who came here on this occasion?'

'Half the neighbourhood.' I held my breath. 'The guy from the Pakistani embassy? The one with the turban?'

'Think about it!'

One of the neighbours, but who? 'The stupid Swede across the road?'

'But that's a teenager.'

'The Persian guy, with the house full of Siamese cats?'

'Never saw him.'

'But he was here.'

She started to get impatient. 'It's not him.'

'Then I don't know. Unless it's one of the firemen.'

'Finally! You're getting warmer.'

'Which one?'

'You tell me.'

'The tall blond, of course.'

'Why of course?'

'One of the black guys?'

Then I suddenly saw him in front of me. The one they called the Chief. The one with the report.

'No!' I said in disbelief.

'Yes.'

'The short fat one, who they called the Chief? The bald one?' To this day I ask myself how I could describe Kowalski in this way. Could it have been jealousy? He was only short compared to the giants in his team. Nor was he fat. That he seemed a little massive must have been because of his broad shoulders. And there was no sign of baldness. Maybe his hair was a little thin, but after all he wasn't as young as the others. Certainly Kowalski wasn't a man you would immediately describe as handsome. Today I might describe him as 'erotic' — like any man who seems to know exactly what he wants to say and wants to do. But back then I was twelve.

'He's not short, or fat, or bald!' Mademoiselle defended him. 'And I have never heard a man with a more exiting voice.'

'In any case, he's pig ugly,' I said, full of spite.

Obviously Mademoiselle had decided not to take my taste as far as men were concerned too seriously. 'His name is Nikolas, by the way. I saw his name on the copy of the report. Nikolas Kowalski.'

For a while we didn't say anything. I thought she was just allowing herself a joke. 'You're joking, right?'

'No, Carlitos, it's true. I have always said that you'd know immediately if you'd met the right man.'

'But he isn't the right man!' Maybe it was the effect of the alcohol, but I was shouting now.

'Yes, darling, he is.'

'He treated you like dirt! Like a criminal!'

'It was his duty. I could have been one of these people who set things on fire just for fun. But the trial will be soon. No doubt he'll be called as a witness.'

I was devastated. 'A short ugly fireman. You can't be serious!'

'I am serious.'

'But why him? What makes him different from all the others?'

Mademoiselle smiled dreamily. 'He's a man.'

* * *

The next day I stayed in bed until noon, and that afternoon I did everything not to run into her. But my mother had long been of the opinion that we spoke too much English and she decreed that Mademoiselle would give me at least three hours of French lessons a day until the end of the Christmas vacation.

If Mademoiselle had hoped that we would continue our conversation about her adored fireman — possibly even in French — she was disappointed. I concentrated strictly on the subject of my lessons and when she once turned the conversation, as if by coincidence, to a burning car, I remained completely unmoved.

'*Carlitos, écoute: tu te promènes à travers Paris et tu vois une voiture qui brûle. Qu'est-ce que tu fais?*'

'I have a look whether someone is sitting in the burning car.'

'And if there isn't? *S'il n'y a personne?*'

'Then I look for a telephone box.'

'*En français.*'

'*Je cherche une . . .* '

' *. . . cabine de téléphone. Et alors?*'

'I call the police.'

'*Tu appelles la police?*'

But for some reason the word for fire department just wouldn't come to me. '*J'appelle les hommes qui tuent le feu.*'

'*Et comment s'appellent-ils, ces hommes?*'

'Firemen.'

'*En français,*' she reprimanded kindly.

'*Les pompiers?*'

'*Bravo!*' Mademoiselle praised me, her pebble-grey eyes smiling at me.

But she couldn't have been more wrong if she expected me to smile back at her conspiratorially. There was not the slightest reason why I should talk to her about the fire department. Had she paid any attention to my invention?

Which brings me to friendship, one of the other themes that preoccupied me back then. What if even friendship was actually a hypocritical relationship, maybe even the most hypocritical relationship of all? You can tell me about your fireman if you listen to me talk about my invention. Call me if you feel lonely, even in the middle of the night, because after all I'd do the same to you. And if you go through a bad patch, I'll give you money, as I know that you'd make any sacrifice for me.

People always say that friendship is the noblest of all human feelings. Nobler than love, which after all is based primarily on our reproductive instinct. Nobler than family ties, which concern people we didn't even pick ourselves. Nobler than our care for the needy, with which we only want to prove that we are kind.

Yet isn't this much-praised friendship precisely the most cold-blooded of all inter-human businesses? Isn't it nothing more than a private contract against those emergencies which official insurance companies can't protect us from? He has dozens of friends, we say about someone, full of admiration. But maybe he is just cunning enough to insure himself properly? He has not one friend, we say contemptuously about someone else. Yet isn't it daring how he walks through life unprotected?

Once, still back in Lima, I had spoken to my mother about this issue. I had just met Stanislav and was so happy to finally have found someone with whom I could talk about everything. But my mother only said that it's better not to think too much about these things. Otherwise I'd become like a centipede which, if it paid constant attention to its feet, would no longer be able to walk.

* * *

On Friday night, my father returned from the office a little earlier than usual. 'Good news!' he shouted, still in the hall. He entered the library and walked up to the table where, with Mademoiselle's help, I was just translating an article from the *Washington Post* into French.

'Especially good news for you, Mademoiselle.' He put a letter on the table. 'It's from the court.'

'From the court?'

'No trial! Obviously the fireman's report about the whole incident was so positive that one didn't feel it necessary to start proceedings.'

She looked at him flabbergasted. 'There will be no trial?'

'I thought you'd be pleased?'

'But of course I'm pleased, monsieur. Thank you.'

When he had left, she picked up the letter and got up. 'Enough for today. *Ça suffit*.'

'But we haven't finished.'

'We'll continue tomorrow.'

I didn't understand it at the time, but for

her a trial was the only realistic hope of ever seeing him again.

✾

School started again the following Monday. I could hardly wait to ask Mrs Lindner, the physics teacher, for her opinion about my invention. She wasn't actually *my* physics teacher. There were no physics lessons at Georgetown Day School in my grade, but she always had an open ear for my problems. And she didn't disappoint me on this occasion.

When I had told her about it, she laughed at me kindly. 'Haven't you heard of the famous Boy Scout experiment?'

'Which Boy Scout experiment?'

'The one with the paper bag. You take a paper bag — a sturdy one, of course — fill it with water and hold it over a fire. What do you think will happen? It should burn, of course! The water would empty over the fire and extinguish it. Well, actually it's just the opposite. The fire leaves the bag intact and the water even comes to the boil.'

'That's not true!'

'Come to the lab. I'll show you.'

She showed me. In the lab, above a Bunsen burner. When after a while the water actually started to boil, tears started running from my eyes.

* * *

Of course that wasn't the first time one of my inventions turned out, after closer investigation, to be just a fantasy. But today I know that at least on occasion I was being ridiculed without reason. In Lima I had invented a flashing dog collar with which you could walk your dog at night and still see where it was. Stanislav told me that no one would buy such a thing as it was forbidden to walk your dog without a leash, and no dog owner would want to expose himself as a lawbreaker. Twenty years later I saw a dog, who answered to the name Kuki, with just such a collar, on a beach in Barcelona. Another time, inspired by Einstein's theory of relativity, I thought of a religion which functioned without bribes — in other words, the faithful wouldn't have to be promised eternal life in paradise to make them behave well on earth. I don't want to go into any detail at this point, but I still think to this day that the whole thing could be a success.

Occasionally my inventions were pure genius but I was trying to break open an open door. For example, I once invented a battery-operated window cleaning apparatus for our maid. When I had finished explaining it to the assembled staff, Franca fetched a rotating wiper from the broom cupboard that had just the qualities that I had thought would bring freedom to all harassed housewives. It took me days to get over my narcissistic hurt. It only got better when I had another, in my opinion, even more spectacular idea. Me and my inventions were like unrequited love, Franca always used to say. Neither travel nor psychotherapy could cure disappointment. There is only one way to forget a man, and that is another man.

* * *

On this occasion the release from my disappointment came that very evening. I went to the ballet with my mother, not voluntarily, it goes without saying. My mother loved the ballet, but I couldn't appreciate what the audience saw — the pleasure of the weightlessness of the human body, the amazement at the infinite possibilities of moving our limbs. To me, watching ballet just made it apparent how futile it is for a person to practise hopping around for decades. Ultimately she hops one, maybe two metres higher than the others, but in the end she crashes to the ground just like the rest of us — there's no sign of weightlessness. And the thing about the infinite movements of the human body is even more of a myth: two arms and two legs which move in every direction make it all the more evident how few possibilities there really are. Later, when I got to find out about sex, I was similarly disappointed. The whole world pretends that there are hundreds of exciting possibilities, but in the end there are no more than four or five positions which are truly satisfying. Anyhow, for me ballet was nothing more than an aerobics class that you had to pay admission to watch. And accordingly I thought of the people who did so as stupid.

On this occasion, my mother didn't have to wait long for my outburst. 'I appreciate that they're having fun. But couldn't they perform their gymnastics in a place where no one has to watch?'

'Darling . . . ' my mother whispered.

'Stravinski! It's a shame for the music.'

My mother pushed her elbow in my direction energetically, and left her arm on the armrest as a warning. I looked at her hand. It was well groomed, with perfectly painted fingernails. Between her thumb and index finger she held the programme notes, which I had read to her before the performance, as out of vanity she of course didn't have her reading glasses with her. ('Should I walk around looking like an automobile?') Yet she openly wore the thick golden bracelet from India with an elephant herd engraved on it. In her place I would have preferred to tie the reading glasses around my arm.

My heart missed a beat: glasses around the wrist! Of course, that's it! No, not glasses, but a magnifying glass you could take off whenever necessary. On the right wrist a magnifying glass, the left a wristwatch. But why so complicated? You could combine the magnifying glass with the watch and make it one apparatus, worn on the left wrist. And what a huge demand there would be for my invention! Everyone who constantly gets worked up about not being able to find their reading glasses — and that must be as good as everyone over the age of forty-five — would be thrilled about my invention. Of course you wouldn't use it to read books, but you would always be prepared for emergencies: the deciphering of a programme, a menu in a restaurant, a price tag in a supermarket, a timetable, a telephone number. All that would no longer pose a problem.

That same night I made a sketch. I have kept it all those years as this invention was the last 'normal' thing for me. The end of my innocence, so to speak. Maybe even the end of my childhood. And it is only preserved because I sent it to Stanislav for her opinion, for nothing in the sky-blue house on Olive Street escaped the fire.

✾

On Tuesday afternoon it was time for my piano lesson with Mr Pilgrim again, to which Mademoiselle had to accompany me, as well as pick me up after an hour.

I hated Mr Pilgrim's piano lessons. I didn't have anything against playing piano as such, just the opposite. When I was five years old, we had spent the summer vacation in the house of friends of my parents in Civitavecchia, a harbour town close to Rome, where my father was employed at the embassy at the time. The hosts noticed that I was able to identify the approaching ships long before they appeared by the sound their engines made. When we had returned to the city, my parents dragged me to a music professor who promptly discovered my musical talents were well above average and since then I had piano lessons wherever we lived.

I don't know how my mother found Mr

Pilgrim of all people. Maybe it was just because he lived nearby and we therefore didn't have to use the driver. That day Mademoiselle and I were once again on our way to the lesson and I was thinking whether I should tell her about my problem with this piano teacher. And I didn't even know whether it was actually a problem, as he was already over seventy and in my book totally geriatric. He was a thin, tall man with a pointed nose and grey hair that grew down to his shoulders and was parted precisely in the middle. But he had a habit that irritated me more and more. Like my teacher in Lima he usually sat next to me on my right on the piano bench. Yet as soon as he sat down, as if by accident, he put his bony hand on my right knee. And whenever he turned over a new page of the sheet music, it moved, again as if by accident, a few centimetres further up my thigh. This never went so far that you really could have accused him of anything in particular, but somehow I had begun to find his touches more and more revolting. In any case, I had become used to putting on two pairs of trousers for my piano lessons, one on top of the other. As you can imagine, my concentration on playing the piano wasn't as good as it might have been. I had to be prepared at any moment, just in case he dared to go a little bit further.

As far as his selection of exercises was concerned, Mr Pilgrim was also quite original: Johann Sebastian Bach, nothing else was on the menu. 'The only one!' he used to say. 'The only one whom it's worth learning the piano for!' He then pointed at a bust of the master that was placed near the window as if as a warning. To this day, the hours I spent in this teacher's filthy, tobacco-reeking summer house have bizarre repercussions as far as my taste in music is concerned. I must be the only person in the world for whom Bach's ascetic compositions trigger sexual associations.

* * *

Just as I was beginning to muster my courage to tell Mademoiselle about my problem with Mr Pilgrim, it was she who started to speak. 'Carlitos, let's assume you've fallen in love with an Air France pilot . . . '

'Air France?'

'Aerolineas Argentinas if you prefer. But this pilot is not aware of your love. Maybe he doesn't even know that you exist. You will have to find a way to see him again. What would you do?'

I thought about it. 'OK, first I'd buy myself

a ticket. For the route he flies. Once we were airborne I'd give the stewardess a hundred dollars and tell her that I had to get to the pilot's cabin, because . . . '

'And assuming you'd fallen in love with an architect?'

'I'd pretend to be rich and would get him to design a house for me.'

Mademoiselle sighed deeply. 'And what about a fireman? Assuming it's a fireman you wanted to see again?'

The thought was so grotesque that I almost didn't dare speak it: 'With a fireman, I'd burn something.'

'What would you burn? A house?'

'What else?'

'*Voilà!*'

We had arrived at Mr Pilgrim's garden gate.

'Don't you want to come inside? You could wait for me?'

'I'll be back in an hour. I have to think.'

* * *

We didn't talk about the matter further. But a few evenings later — my parents had flown to Los Angeles and were due back the following day — three trash cans not more than fifty metres from our house caught fire.

I had already fallen asleep when Mademoiselle stormed into my room. '*Réveille-toi*, Charlotte!'

'What happened?'

'There's a fire.'

'Again?' I leapt out of bed.

'But no, not here. There . . . ' She opened the window, brushed the snow from the windowsill so I could lean outside. At some distance, I could see the silhouette of something from which reddish smoke was emerging. I turned to her aghast.

'It's only a couple of trash cans,' she reassured me, smiling.

'And you . . . '

'Who else? But you'll have to make the call. My accent is too noticeable.'

We ran down to the drawing room and Mademoiselle dialled the number of the fire department, which by this time she of course knew by heart. When she handed me the receiver she covered it with her hand. 'Don't tell them your name. And don't tell them that it's trash cans, otherwise they won't take it seriously.'

A male voice answered. 'Washington Fire Department.'

I could feel my heart pounding. 'Is that the fire service?'

'What's up?'

'I'm calling from Olive Street. Olive Street, Georgetown. Around the corner from N Street, where the President used to live.'

'Which president?'

'The President of the United States.'

'Are you trying to kid me?' the man on duty asked, laughing kindly. God knows how many crank calls they get every day.

'I'm telling you, because there's a fire!' I put the receiver down.

'Fantastic! You've done great, *chérie*!' She kissed me on both cheeks, French style.

Only now I noticed that she was wearing the white silk negligee my father had given my mother for Christmas. And underneath the matching silk nightie, both by Dior.

'But that's my mother's negligee.'

'I'm only borrowing it. I have to be pretty when he comes. And it has to look as if I was disturbed in deep sleep.'

She unravelled her knotted hair, walked over to the mirror and looked at herself from all angles.

'How do I look?'

It was the first time I saw her concerned about her appearance.

'Good.' I was still a little sleepy.

'Or maybe I should get her blue housecoat?' She was still standing in front of the mirror. 'Or the chequered one? Tell me!'

'It would be warmer.'

'Warmer! *Ce sont les apparances qui comptent!*'

I let her suffer a little longer. 'The white one's OK!'

* * *

When the fire trucks turned into our street, we ran outside as if attracted by the sirens. Mademoiselle had made sure that I was wearing the winter coat with a hood over my pyjamas, but she went just as she was: who thinks of their health when there is a fire at their neighbour's? She couldn't have known that it was only a couple of trash cans. They were blazing by now. I wondered how she had done it.

The other neighbours had also come out of their houses. You could see that some of them weren't sure what deserved more attention: the burning rubbish or my nanny looking as if she'd escaped from a Hollywood movie. Like three weeks previously, there were again two trucks, and the crew was also the same, even the beautiful blond guy was amongst them. He was the first to jump off the truck to connect the hose to the hydrant. If only it was him she had picked! I thought.

After a few moments of panic, we also

discovered Nick Kowalski, who directed the somewhat comical operation of extinguishing the burning trash cans with a few efficient gestures. However, on this occasion it took a little longer than it had with our tree: just when you thought that the matter was dealt with, some more flames flared up.

'How did you do it?' I asked Mademoiselle quietly.

'Yesterday they collected old clothes.'

'What's that got . . . '

'I lit three packets of these spirit tablets, the ones Americans use to light their barbecues, and put them in three bags full of old clothes. And then I put them into the three containers, with the lid open, of course.'

'Oxygen,' I said expertly.

'Precisely.'

'And when they analyse the remains? What about the labels?'

'*Tu me prends pour une débile?* I wouldn't take clothes from our house!' And when I remained quietly impressed. 'Good, no?'

'Not bad.'

As it was icy cold, the other spectators soon returned to their houses one by one. Some had tried to strike up a conversation with Mademoiselle, but quickly realised that she wasn't in the mood. She stood very upright in the middle of the street. A small gust of wind blew her white silk coat. She looked like a magnificent sailboat stranded in Antarctica.

When Nick Kowalski signalled the end of the matter with a quick lifting of his hands, she was of course immediately surrounded by the entire fire crew, who looked at her in admiration, full of reverence. She had just taken me by the hand and pretended that it was time for us too to return, when Nick Kowalski finally also approached.

'Old friends,' he laughed. And to me: 'This time we managed without you, did you see that?'

'Yes, isn't that odd?' Mademoiselle replied instead of me. 'Two fires in the same street, only three weeks apart.'

'The law of the series,' Kowalski said.

'The law of the series?' Mademoiselle dug deeper. She looked completely calm, but as she was still holding my hand I could feel her shiver with excitement — but also probably a little with the cold. If he left now, everything would have been in vain.

'Well, these things usually happen in . . . ' He looked for the right word, but failed. 'Well, in series.'

'You'll have to explain that to me,' Mademoiselle said excitedly. 'I find the world of the fire department fascinating!'

Nick Kowalski looked her over, bemused: 'I

think you'd better get back into your warm bed, miss. You'll catch pneumonia.' He turned around. 'Lieutenant?'

The handsome blond stepped up. 'Chief?'

'Get a blanket.'

'Yes, Chief.'

Mademoiselle made a desperate attempt to continue the conversation. 'The proceedings have been discontinued.'

'Which proceedings?'

'Against me.'

'Really? Then you know more than me. But surely it didn't get very far in the first place?'

'Yes, that's what I wanted to say. I'm sure I have your report to thank.'

'Which was completely objective.'

'Do you think I'm incapable of lighting a fire? I mean just for fun?'

Nick Kowalski looked at her calmly. 'I'm sure you've started a few fires in your time.' The whole crew was laughing.

In the meantime the blond had returned. 'The blanket, Chief.'

'Put it around the two ladies and take them back to their house.' And to Mademoiselle: 'The lieutenant will explain the law of the series to you.'

'Why not me?' one of the black firemen laughed.

'Why not all of us?' another laughed.

Kowalski stopped the laughter with a brief gesture. And then he turned away. From Mademoiselle!

* * *

We returned home in silence, handed back the woollen blanket to the blond at the front door in silence, entered the house in silence, where Mademoiselle peeled me out of my coat in silence. And then she took me in her arms and whirled with me through the entire ground floor.

'Isn't he fantastic? Isn't he wonderful? Did you see his eyes, Carlitos? Did you notice the way he talked? Not one word too much! And his accent!'

I swear that's the truth. Every other woman would have given up after such a fiasco. First this stupid fireman ignored her, then he ridiculed her. He left her standing in the middle of a conversation and, by asking the best-looking crew member to accompany her home, practically drove her into the arms of someone else. After all, she'd only have had to invite the blond in and he would have been hers. And what did she do? She behaved as if she had scored a victory!

Eventually she put me down on my feet again. It was my turn to talk. 'He's an idiot!

He treated you like dirt!'

'*Mais non*,' she laughed.

'*Mais non?* He couldn't have made it clearer that he's not interested in you.'

'That's precisely it. Should he fall over just because a pretty French girl stands in front of him in a night-gown? He's exactly what I need. A man with principles! A woman needs a man she can rely on, not someone who runs after the next good-looking girl.'

'He practically handed you to another man.'

'He wanted to test me.'

I was speechless.

'Carlitos, you don't yet understand these things, you're just a child. But I swear that he'll call me. Maybe not tomorrow, but the day after tomorrow at the latest. Want to bet?'

I thought about it. Maybe she was right? After all, in the three months I'd known her, I hadn't seen a single man being ambivalent towards her.

'You'll see,' she said triumphantly. 'He'll call me and invite me to take a look round his fire station.'

* * *

But Nick Kowalski didn't call. Not the next day, not the day after that. He didn't call all week.

'Maybe he's sick?' she said meekly after a few days. 'Carlitos, couldn't you call the fire station and ask for him? Say it's a personal matter. And if he comes to the phone, hang up.'

I used the phone in my father's study, where you could listen in with a second receiver. They didn't ask me any questions, and called him immediately. 'A lady for you,' I heard someone say in the background, followed by the laughter of a group of men. Then he came to the telephone, called himself Nick. Mademoiselle gave me a sign and I hung up.

'At least now we know that he's not sick,' she said. But she said it in a tone of voice that suggested that she'd have preferred it if he were dead. Better dead than not interested in Mademoiselle.

'Maybe it was a different Nick?'

'It was him. I'd recognise his voice among millions.'

'And what do we do now?' I was the one who asked the question.

'No idea.' She sounded close to tears.

'We'll just go over there. We say that we're interested in the fire station. Ask him to explain how everything works.'

'Impossible.'

'But why?'

'*C'est hors de question.*'

'How else are you going to see him again?'

'No idea, but not that way. The number one rule for every woman: the man always has to make the first step.'

'Who says?'

'My father.'

'The one with the night-club?'

'Running a night-club gives you a lot of experience. There were six of us girls, so he made up six rules for us. Rule number one is that the man is the hunter, the woman the hunted.'

'I'm not the hunted.'

'But you have to pretend to be. Men like it that way. The real men. If you turn the whole thing on its head and they get the impression that they're the ones being hunted, it doesn't work any more. Maybe you get some kind of man, my father says, but not a real man.'

'But if real men are so stupid, is it worth making so much effort?'

'I asked my father the same question. He said that in the end every woman would have to decide that for herself, but that there is no other way. *Voilà*.'

* * *

The next few days we hardly spoke. It was as if Mademoiselle wasn't there. At our meals together she ate her food listlessly. I couldn't get the problem out of my head either: surely there must be some solution? After all, the fire department didn't only come when there was a fire, but also in other emergencies. A burst pipe, for example — maybe we should flood the basement? But that would be too heartless towards my parents, who hadn't yet managed to recover from the flood at Christmas. Maybe a burst pipe in one of the empty houses in the neighbourhood? But who would discover it? A kitten trapped on top of a tree? How would we get it up there? And we'd probably have to tie it on a branch to keep it there. And in any case it was unlikely that the chief of the fire department would turn up for such a rescue operation. After all he was who the whole thing was about.

At times, we began to bicker with each other.

'One shouldn't cut potatoes with a knife!'

'But it's easier.'

'But it's wrong.'

'How should you know? You aren't a real nanny.'

'I'm not? So what do I get paid for?'

I was inattentive at school and even my mother noticed that I was more pensive than usual.

'Carlota, what's the matter? If you have a problem, you should tell me. I'm your mother.'

'I have a problem. But I can't talk about it.'

'Is it one of your inventions?'

'Yes.'

'Can't you talk to your physics teacher about it? She's helped you many times before.'

'That is a good idea.'

'You see!' She kissed me on the top of my head. 'By the way, I like your pigtails better every day.'

I held the ends of the pigtails under my nose like a moustache. 'Why don't you come over and play with Caroline some time?'

She gave me a friendly pat on the back. 'Cheeky brat!'

* * *

What could I have told her? The problem was how to bewitch an American fireman according to the rules of a French night-club owner. To bewitch, to conquer, to marry and to make children with him.

I wrote a long letter to my friend Stanislav. I told her about Christmas and the tree incident. I described my invention with the magnifying glass to her in great detail and asked her to tell me honestly if she thought it was nonsense. And in the postscript I asked her a question: 'Presume you had fallen madly in love with a fireman and had to see him again. What would you do? And please don't tell me you'd set your house on fire. I am looking for serious advice.'

* * *

The next day it was time for Mr Pilgrim's piano lesson again and as usual Mademoiselle accompanied me. We talked about everything under the sun except what really interested us. Nick Kowalski wasn't mentioned once.

'You're depressed, Carlitos,' Mademoiselle finally said. As if I was the only one who was depressed!

'The stupid piano lessons. They're getting on my nerves.'

'But everyone says you're so talented. Your mother thinks you'll be a great pianist one day.'

'I'd prefer to walk the streets.'

'Charlotte!' she complained, without much enthusiasm.

'But it's true.'

'As a pianist you get to travel.'

'Travel!' I pretended to throw up.

'Thousands of people will applaud you.'

'Yes, but before that happens I'll have to sit on a piano stool for a hundred years! All pianists are idiots. Anyone halfway intelligent wouldn't stand sitting eight hours every day on a little stool, tinkling off the same old stuff, over and over again. And when they're finished with it, they play the same thing again in front of perfect strangers and let themselves be celebrated for it. If they'd at least composed the stuff themselves! But all they can do is play the piano by heart. It's only logical that the better they play, the more stupid they must be. After all they had to practise longer for the applause.'

'You're impossible!' Mademoiselle laughed.

When was the last time I had heard her laugh?

We arrived at the iron gate, which opened to the path leading through Mr Pilgrim's garden to the wooden pavilion, where, hidden away from the neighbours, he held his curious lessons.

'Don't you want to come in?' I begged. 'Who knows how long until our grand piano finally gets here from Lima. You can listen to me play!'

'Another time, Carlitos. Now I have to think, OK?'

Think! She'd walk along M Street, cross Georgetown Bridge and pass the fire station on the opposite side of the street. Obviously according to her father's rules a chance meeting was allowed. But Nick Kowalski didn't look like the sort of guy who goes for a walk during his break. But at least she'd have been close to him.

* * *

The next day when we were on our way to M Street to buy some rare spices for Franca, I started to talk about it. 'We'll need a third one.'

'A third what?'

'A third fire.'

'*Tu es folle!*'

'No, I thought about it. If we have to stick to your father's rules, there's no other possibility.'

'Two fires should've been enough.'

'But they weren't enough. You saw so for yourself.'

'Do you want me to burn down half of Georgetown just to meet a fireman again?'

'What if it's the only way?'

She stopped and grabbed me by the shoulders. 'Charlotte, I don't ever want to hear you say that again. Is that understood?'

* * *

But a couple of days later, on another walk she had suggested out of the blue, we began to discuss carefully the practical possibilities. It was as if Mademoiselle had come back to life.

'It can't be in our street again,' she said.

'Why not? The law of the series.'

'They wouldn't buy that from us.'

'So not in Georgetown.'

'Of course in Georgetown.'

'But what if they catch on?'

'It's likely that another fire station is responsible for other districts. No, it'll have to be in this district. But not too close to Olive Street.'

'In that case, it would have to be a larger fire.'

'Why?'

'So we have an excuse to be there. No one runs ten blocks because of a burning trash can.'

She nodded thoughtfully. 'You're right.'

'And the noise would have to be so loud that you could, at least in theory, hear it in Olive Street. So we'd need a larger object, where they'd need the help of additional fire departments from surrounding areas.'

'There'd have to be another condition,' Mademoiselle said.

'OK.'

'It has to be in Georgetown, a larger fire, but still completely harmless. No one should have to be afraid. Not even a cat, you hear me? I wouldn't be able to survive if someone came to harm!'

For a while we walked along in silence.

'I've got it,' I said.

'What?'

'An idea of what to burn.'

This time it was me who took her by the hand. We ran a further four blocks along the street and then arrived at the canal, out of breath. There she was: the *Georgetown Queen*, a large, dilapidated wooden boat, covered with a blue plastic awning. If we managed to light this monstrosity, we'd have it made. We wouldn't even have to call the fire department ourselves. The Chesapeake and Ohio Canal, as it was called, was lined with beautiful family houses. And when the fire engines arrived, from every direction, we'd run to the canal just like all the other inhabitants.

'And there'd be no danger!' Mademoiselle shouted, still breathless after our run. 'It's on the water! And the owner would probably be glad to get rid of the old thing. Carlitos, you're unbelievable!'

* * *

And now life became really interesting. Of course I wasn't required to come up with an invention as such, but finally my technical know-how was called for. Over the next few days I again and again sneaked past the boat. I had forbidden Mademoiselle to accompany me, as anonymity was impossible as far as she was concerned.

I measured the length of the *Georgetown Queen* with my steps: it was approximately twenty-three metres long. It must've been about six metres wide. And even though most of it was made of wood, we'd have to get at least two canisters of petrol to make sure that this mammoth burned properly.

Petrol. Under no circumstances could we be seen buying it. Imagine a twelve-year-old at a gas station. 'Five gallons of petrol, please.' An hour after the fire, I'd be sitting in Georgetown's police station, in handcuffs.

What I did buy was a one-and-a-half-metre-long plastic pipe, about as thick as my index finger. The evening before the 'crime', while my parents were having dinner with their guests, I used it to suck two big canisters' worth of petrol out of their cars. One from my father's Mercedes limousine, the other from my mother's Ford Coupé. 'Who do you like better, Mummy or Daddy?' Well, in this case, neither of them would feel left out.

Mademoiselle was leaning against the wall of the garage, silently. She was wearing her denim suit, and followed every one of my movements.

'I can't let you get involved in this,' she finally said.

'And why not?'

'You're a child.'

'*Et alors?*'

'I'm paid to look after you. Not to teach you how to set boats on fire.'

'And how were you planning to teach me that? You don't even know how to do it yourself.'

The flow of petrol from my father's car was interrupted. That's what happens when you have a conversation while doing these things! I had to suck the pipe full again and suddenly my mouth was full of petrol.

'Carlitos, you're only twelve!'

I matter-of-factly spat the petrol out on the ground. 'That's another advantage. I can't yet be prosecuted.'

'They'll get your father.'

'He has immunity.'

'He has what?'

'Diplomatic status. They can't do anything to him. And the worst they can do to me is send me to a shrink twice a week, which would be much more amusing than Mr Pilgrim's piano lessons.'

When she didn't say anything, I looked up at her. 'They won't catch us. I swear.'

* * *

Three days later, at around seven o'clock in the morning, we embarked on our project. It was a Sunday and, as far as we were concerned, the perfect day of the week for our purpose. First, there were no staff at the house, and secondly, my parents never got up before noon that day. In any case, their bedroom looked out on the garden.

The owner and landlord of our house in Olive Street was a black diplomat, to whom John F. Kennedy had given some embassy as soon as he was in office, presumably somewhere in Africa. He obviously had several children as I had discovered masses of toys in one of the rooms in the basement. I had also found a well-preserved baby carriage, which we now took to the garage, along with a doll the size of a new-born baby, with dark skin. We dusted the baby carriage and deposited the two petrol canisters at the bottom. On top of it we put the baby doll, covered it carefully and lowered the little curtain attached at the head of the carriage.

Anywhere else, people would wonder about a white, pigtailed twelve-year-old taking her black brother for a walk. But in Georgetown no one would pay any attention.

Of course Mademoiselle wanted to accompany me. She had seen the film *Wages of Fear* and now seemed to think that the slightest movement could make my cargo blow me up like Yves Montand's colleague's truck full of nitroglycerine. However, I insisted on doing the excursion on my own. On Sunday, there was not a soul on the streets, not even a car. So as not to raise any suspicion, I bent down to my little brother from time to time and talked to him with a loving smile. 'Hey, little black guy! Why don't you crawl over to the White House and play with Caroline?' If someone had been looking out of the window by chance, they'd count themselves lucky to start the day witnessing such an enchanting display of sisterly love.

It was also very plausible for me to turn off after the bridge and choose the footpath. Where else would you go for a walk with a baby on a Sunday morning? By now, it was March and there was no sign of ice or snow, and the sun had even appeared from behind the clouds. I casually walked up to the undergrowth next to the *Georgetown Queen*, and turned into it with my baby carriage. I quickly removed the doll, lugged the two petrol canisters out and onto the ground and hid them underneath some branches which I had collected and assembled there the day before. Then I replaced the doll, covered it and navigated the baby carriage back out onto the footpath. For appearance's sake, I adjusted my clothes. If someone had observed me from a window, they'd assume that the little sweetheart had to do its business behind the bushes. I leisurely continued my walk. Mademoiselle awaited me in Olive Street, next to the open garage door. She looked pale.

* * *

Then came Sunday evening. The conditions were ideal, as my parents had accepted an invitation to spend the evening in a country house next to some lake far outside Washington. Even if they found out about the fire and became worried, it'd be two hours before they could be back in Georgetown.

This time it was also me who set out first. The plan was that Mademoiselle would follow me at some distance and wait for me at the bridge. Now I only had a bag with me, in it my father's Swiss army knife, a box of Mademoiselle's French matches, as well as two torches I had found in the changing cabin — no doubt left over from some garden party — which I had shortened to thirty centimetres. And of course I was wearing my high Wellington boots, which fortunately were black and therefore completely inconspicuous.

'Her heart was in her mouth.' When I was reaching for the two canisters in the darkness, I finally knew what this hackneyed expression really meant. But Mademoiselle and I had rehearsed often enough by the pool, so that, even with a fluttering pulse, I was able to complete my assignment. It was pitch dark and, as it was almost midnight, only a few windows of the houses alongside the canal were lit. I took the first canister and felt my way through the bushes to the canal. Luckily the boat was close enough to the bank, so that five steps in the shallow water were enough to reach and climb onto it.

I took out my Swiss army knife, slit open the blue plastic awning far enough for me to lower myself and the canister through the hole and onto the wooden floor of the deck. Protected by the cover, I crawled on my knees over the planks like a midnight cleaning woman, sparingly but systematically distributing my inflammable liquid. After my deed was done, I crawled back to where I got in, and enlarged the small slit to an opening a square metre large, through which I could throw a torch from the bank.

I jumped off the boat and felt my way back to the hiding place to fetch the second canister, the contents of which I emptied directly over the boat, walking around it in the shallow water. I had left the first canister behind on the boat and once I had finished with the second one, I also threw it onto the *Georgetown Queen*. Then I waded back to the bank, lit a torch with Mademoiselle's matches and, from a distance of about three metres, threw it onto the boat, exactly into the opening I had prepared for it. I had planned to use the second torch to light the petrol floating on the water, but I quickly realised that this wouldn't be necessary: after a couple of seconds everything was ablaze.

As arranged, I now ran far enough from the fire to be safe, stopped and screamed 'Fire!' as loudly as I could into the silence of this exclusive neighbourhood. As I was running away, I could see out of the corner of my eyes lights coming on in the houses on both sides of the canal and windows being thrown open. Now there were others shouting 'Fire!'

Mademoiselle waited for me with wide-open arms on the dark bridge, and silently pulled me against her soft, shivering body.

* * *

What does it feel like to look at a fire you started yourself — a fire of this size? Well, in this case a cliché springs to mind: the feeling is 'indescribable'. No, it's not a feeling of happiness. And neither is it one of euphoria. Perhaps it's one of power? Perhaps that comes closer, but that still would only be one aspect of it. After all, although you started this magnificent inferno, you'd be unable to stop it. Maybe you could say: it is a feeling of power and powerlessness at the same time, and both in their most extreme form. Later, I occasionally found this contradiction in the arms of a man: maybe it was I who caused his passion, but now I powerlessly submitted to him. Maybe that's why experts mention arson and eroticism in the same breath. Since that year with Mademoiselle, I have failed to encounter something as monumental in any other area of life.

She stood next to me on the bridge, where more and more people had started to assemble. Overwhelmed, outraged witnesses to this destruction, and us, the guilty ones, right there amongst them. Did I feel guilty? Not in the slightest: the feeling that arose in me was more like pride, for it was indeed a magnificent fire.

Then I heard the first siren — as far as I was concerned far too soon — and then a second, a third. Soon it sounded like an open-air concert spread across Georgetown. The first fire engines started to arrive on the opposite bridge — not as we had anticipated, but actually quite logically, as it was at least twenty metres closer to the fire. The first firemen were jumping off the trucks.

'Come,' Mademoiselle said. When I couldn't tear myself away she added: 'We have to be one of the first. He has to see us!'

So we ran as fast as we could to the other bridge. In the meantime the fire engines' floodlights had been lit and a couple of firemen had quickly erected a barrier to keep back the onlookers. We were standing right behind it, waiting for Nick Kowalski to appear. Soon there were so many onlookers that we found it difficult to keep our places in the front row. Everyone admired the extent of the fire — which, by the way, wasn't nearly as impressive in the bright lights — and chatted excitedly. When it became apparent that no one was in danger in the abandoned old boat, the onlookers began to theorise about the possible motive: it must have been the owner who wanted to cash in on the insurance. As many of them were wearing nightgowns and pyjamas under their coats and knew each other at least by sight, a lively atmosphere quickly materialised. It was almost like being at a midnight fair.

There was a problem even I, the mastermind behind it all, hadn't thought of: the path next to the canal was too small and therefore none of the trucks could drive right up to the fire. Of course, there was as much water as you could have wanted, and the danger of the fire spreading was also nil. But it took a while before the men managed to direct an effective water jet onto my creation, to be able to start to extinguish it.

I smelled the sleeve of my winter coat: it stank of petrol.

But where was Kowalski? As much as we turned our heads, he was nowhere to be seen.

'Everything was in vain, Carlitos,' Mademoiselle said, in my opinion much too loudly. 'He's not here.'

'Impossible,' I whispered back. 'With a fire this size? They'll need every man!'

I pushed myself through to the fireman who was in charge of the barrier. 'Excuse me, sir, could you tell me where Nick is?'

'Nick?' He turned around and pointed at a black guy who was busy at the back of the fire engine. 'Over there.'

'Not that Nick. Nick Kowalski!'

'The Chief? What day is it today? Sunday? It's his day off.'

My world collapsed. 'His day off? With a fire like that?'

He grinned. 'Even firemen have to take a day off now and then. And this thing isn't that bad.' He pointed at the site of the fire, which by now had been reduced to smoke. 'Everything's under control. By the way, the lady over there, is she with you? Is she your big sister?'

I returned to Mademoiselle. 'Sunday. His day off.'

She took my hand in silence, and we walked back to Olive Street without her saying a word. At home she helped me get undressed — my boots were full of water — put my pyjamas on and put me to bed. I was dead tired and fell asleep immediately.

Mademoiselle's silence didn't just last the next day, it lasted for weeks. Of course, she still gave me French lessons, and then had to talk to me. She accompanied me to the dentist, to the piano lessons and in the afternoons when I returned from school she waited for me at the corner where my bus stopped. But we didn't mention the night of the fire once. It hadn't occurred to either of us to go to the canal to check what had remained of the boat.

Once when we were sitting at our solitary meal, I looked up and saw that tears were running down her cheeks. She noticed my glance and shouted at me. 'Now just don't say that we need a fourth fire!' It was heartbreaking.

* * *

Apart from that, I can remember little about the weeks after the third fire — and it really already had been three: the Christmas tree, the trash cans and the boat. I have a faint recollection of a dinner at the house of a Democrat senator who lived nearby, to which I had to accompany my father. Maybe it was because he had a son my age, who of course didn't materialise in the end. Someone said he had a cold. I knew it was more likely that he was simply as fed up with the whole matchmaking thing as I was. In any case, the conversation turned to John F. Kennedy and his stance on racial politics, which our host described as 'highly questionable'. If the President didn't clearly distance himself from this Martin Luther King pretty soon, it would cost him millions of votes in the South.

'But Kennedy promised he'd help them!' I protested.

The senator turned to me and smiled. 'Promised that he will help who, young lady?'

'The blacks!'

'That's right, of course. But what if he loses his job in the process? Then he'll be no good to anyone, will he?'

I took a deep breath. 'Well. Only the President of the United States could stop the discrimation against the blacks . . . '

'Discrimination,' my father corrected.

'Only he could stop it. But as that would cost you the white vote, as soon as you're President of the United States, you can't do anything for the blacks.' The whole table shook with laughter.

'My good old Carlota,' my father said, not without pride.

The lady next to me, who was wearing about a hundred golden bracelets, patted my head lovingly. 'Isn't she sweet? These wonderful pigtails! My child, you won't find anyone here who's against equal rights for the coloured.'

All hypocrites, that much I already knew. Of those who visited us driven by their chauffeur — and the chauffeur was always black — no one ever brought him into the house. And I never saw any of our visitors looking at their watches and saying: 'Well, we better go, I'm sure our poor George out there is fed up waiting.' Drivers had to wait, and usually they were black. Presumably they couldn't even read properly, as I never saw one with a book or newspaper while they spent all that time sitting in their car. If there were a few of them, they stood together, and tried to keep themselves warm stamping their feet. If it was only one, he sat in the limousine and just stared into the distance. In this case, I sometimes sneaked out at night and had a little chat with him. No one had ever told on me.

'Agreed?' the woman with the golden bracelets asked.

'I think he's great,' I said defiantly.

'Who do you think is great?'

'Martin Luther King.'

'But we all do,' my father said, closing the subject a little impatiently. Our Washington driver was also black. But as we lived close by, we had walked the few steps that evening.

* * *

A few days later, a letter arrived from Stanislav. Stanislav! At Christmas I thought I couldn't live without her and now it was May and I had almost forgotten about her.

She wrote in detail about my invention, which she found 'not bad'. I should patent it and then — and only then! — get in touch with a glasses manufacturer or, better, a watchmaker. Of course the easiest way would be an open, simple bracelet with a big round magnifying glass, as wide as a woman's wrist. It could be taken off quickly, the woman could hold it like a lorgnon and, if it was finished beautifully, would be able to wear it like a piece of jewellery. But that would only be useful for women, as no real man would ever wear a bracelet. No real man? So it also had got to her. She was a year older than me. Was she in love?

In the postscript she finally turned to my problem with the fireman, and her suggestion wasn't bad. 'Ask him for an interview,' she wrote in her self-assured, adult handwriting. 'No man can resist the temptation to talk about himself. Tell him it's for school. Theme: My Hero.'

I showed Mademoiselle the last part of the letter, who gave it back to me, outraged. '*C'est absolument ridicule*. I have to meet him, not you!'

'Then come with me! We'll tell him my parents won't allow me to go by myself.'

'Impossible.'

'But why not?'

'Only if he insisted on it.'

'And if he doesn't?'

She looked at me. For the first time in weeks there was a glimmer of hope in her eyes. 'Then you go on your own. We'll discuss precisely what you have to ask him. *Tu as compris?*'

* * *

Sometimes you're just lucky. The next day Mrs Cook, our English teacher, announced that we had to write an essay over the summer holidays and asked the class for suggestions for its theme. She hadn't finished speaking when I raised my arm. 'My Hero,' I said.

Her smile, was more than condescending. 'You have obviously found one?'

'Her daddy!' the spotty Ken Fulder burst out behind me, and the whole class brayed with laughter.

'As a theme it isn't bad,' Mrs Cook announced to my surprise. 'Any suggestions?'

'I'd write about the fire department,' I said before someone else could hijack the subject. 'Our Christmas tree caught fire last Christmas,' I added, to establish myself as an expert.

'Very well, Carlota Linares can do the fire department. How about anyone else?'

* * *

Now came the difficult part. I had to ask Nick Kowalski whether he'd give me an interview. I called him straight after school.

'This is Carlota. The one from Olive Street, whose Christmas tree caught fire.'

He remembered instantly. 'Where's the fire this time?'

'Nowhere,' I giggled like an idiot. 'But I wanted to ask . . . I wanted to ask you whether you'd give me an interview. It's for school. I want to write a portrait about you.'

'Theme: My Hero.'

'How did you know?'

Instead of a reply came a laugh. 'Then come over. Do you know where we are?'

'M Street and 23rd. When?'

'How about Friday? At five.'

'Thank you. Thank you very much! . . . Mr Kowalski?'

'What is it?'

'Can I bring Mademoiselle?'

'An interview with a babysitter? I thought that this was between grown-ups?'

'No problem.'

'See you Friday. But only if there's no fire.' He said it without a hint of irony. I began to realise how strange his profession really was.

* * *

I immediately ran down to Mademoiselle in the basement apartment. She was listening to her French records — turned up so loud that I had to ring the bell several times.

'Friday at five!' I shouted triumphantly. She looked at me, not comprehending. 'The interview with Kowalski!'

'You called him?'

'I did.'

'Just like that?'

She looked so astonished that I had to laugh. 'He's only a fireman, not God.'

But as she was in love with him, that's just what he was to her. 'Love is the religion with the smallest congregation,' I once formulated years later, when I took part in a discussion which once again concerned itself with finding a definition for this strange thing. For, compared to other religions, God and devotee were in this case at a ratio of one to one. But it turned out, during my interview of all places, that the god Nick Kowalski, in my eyes so undesirable, was coveted by two women.

* * *

At precisely 5 p.m. next Friday I was standing with Mademoiselle in front of the fire station in M Street. I was in quite a state: we had spent days compiling lists of questions, rejected some, rephrased others, added new ones. On one hand it had to seem that I was actually there because of the essay; on the other, everything had to be tried to establish some sort of private contact at this meeting, or to be precise, an opportunity to see him without having to set something alight. So I was to find out about his hobbies, the restaurants he frequented, his taste in music, whether he liked movies and, if yes, what kind and at which theatres he saw them. If I asked him everything we'd thought of, the interview would take three days.

'So?' Mademoiselle looked at me as if I was leaving for an expedition to the North Pole.

'Why don't you just come with me?'

'Impossible, Carlota.' She gave me a kiss on each cheek. 'But if he asks after me, you can tell him that I'm waiting for you in the café at the corner. You can suggest that you could interview him there. Of course you don't know whether I'd be at all interested.'

I kept it to myself that I had already made a similar suggestion.

* * *

Nick Kowalski. He couldn't have been kinder. He patiently showed me the recently opened facilities, as if he had nothing more important to do in the entire world. He explained why the thick fire hoses hung next to each other from the ceiling instead of being rolled up: they had to be washed and dried after each use. He told me how many manoeuvres they had to go on in an average week, where he differentiated between good and bad weeks. Strangely enough, a good week was when there were a lot of fires to be put out. He made me guess how many fires there were in a city the size of New York every year.

'A thousand . . . Five thousand?'

'Fifty thousand, young lady. No fireman would ever dream of moving into a skyscraper.'

'Where do you live?'

'Foggy Bottom, third floor, roof terrace, fire escape,' he laughed. His laughter seemed to me to be the only truly amazing thing about him, as his eyes turned into small slits while the tips of his eyebrows raised like the devil's. Somehow you immediately got the urge to want to see him laugh again.

He even showed me the crew quarters on the first floor, and he let me slide down the shiny pole which led to the fire engines so that in case of an alarm no valuable time was wasted with stairs. And he described in detail each of the fire engines parked there — the very ones which had come to Olive Street on Christmas Eve, and then again to the burning trash cans. Especially impressive was the truck with the retractable ladder, which could reach up to the fifth floor of a burning building. I remembered that I had a toy that looked very similar when I was four.

'Enough?' he finally asked.

Of course I wanted to ask a hundred more questions about these technical things, but I remembered my mission: 'I still have a few personal questions. Mrs Cook likes that sort of thing in these assignments.'

'Well, come on then. I'll buy you a Coke.'

We went to the recreation room next to the depot, which they called the DFD-Club. At least that's what was written above the door. DFD — the District Fire Department — was also printed on the blue T-shirts everyone was wearing. Four men were sitting around a table, playing cards. One of them was the blond, who greeted me enthusiastically.

'Where's your beautiful nanny today?'

'Mademoiselle is waiting in the cafe at the corner.'

'Wouldn't she be more comfortable waiting here?' He turned to Kowalski. 'Do you want me to get her, Chief?'

'No way. This is a serious interview, right?'

He put a Coke, which he had got from the machine, on the table in front of me. 'Shoot.'

I looked down my list. 'Do you like music?'

'Ludwig van Beethoven,' one of the card players said and spread his little finger graciously.

'You should ask him about his favourite instrument,' his neighbour suggested.

'What's your favourite instrument?'

'The siren!' the other one bawled, earning his colleagues' applause.

'That's enough,' Kowalski said.

'I like French chansons,' I lied. 'Edith Piaf and so on. And you?'

'Let's say Country Music. OK?'

I made a note. 'Do you like movies?'

'Depends. I like Westerns.'

'What do you do in your spare time?'

Now it was the blond who spoke: 'The Chief spends his spare time in the arms of his loved one.' Everyone laughed.

I couldn't believe my ears. 'You have a bride?'

Damn! Why did I use this ridiculous word? Princes had brides, and then only those in fairy tales.

'Luisita Martinez,' the blond said conspiratorially. 'The hairdressing salon on 29th Street. You should ask her about him!'

'I breed pigeons in my spare time,'

Kowalski said, unmoved. 'Carrier pigeons.'

'Carrier pigeons?'

'My father was also a fireman and also bred pigeons. He lives in Poland. Take that down: Polish father, Polish mother.'

'Mexican bride,' the blond added.

Kowalski looked at him, annoyed. 'I was fourteen when I came to America. Next.' But at that moment the alarm rang and everyone jumped up.

Also Nick Kowalski had stood up. 'I'm sorry, young lady, but that comes with the job. Just call me if you need something else. OK?'

I followed them outside. Two men slid down the pole with breathtaking speed, the others were already wearing their boots and jackets, and now took their helmets and ran to their places in the fire engines, which a moment later drove through the now wide-open doors, out onto N Street. Kowalski once again was sitting in the first truck, the one with the water, and waved at me.

I waved back. 'And thank you!' I shouted. But at the same moment the siren sounded.

* * *

I slowly walked over to the cafe. Mademoiselle leapt to her feet when she saw me enter.

'You look like you've got bad news.'

I joined her at the table. 'He breeds pigeons.'

She laughed, relieved. 'Is that all?'

'His father also bred pigeons. His family is Polish.'

'A Pole!' Mademoiselle beamed. 'That explains the accent.' I must have looked really depressed, as she pulled my pigtails, amused. 'But Carlitos, what's the matter? I think that maybe you're a snob. Breeding pigeons is typically working class and all firemen are working class. Everywhere where it can become dangerous — the police, the fire department, the army — it is always the poor who risk their lives for us.'

'He has a fiancee.'

I don't know why she hadn't counted on it just a little. If she liked him so much, it shouldn't have come as a surprise to her that another woman felt the same way.

'Try and think, Charlotte. Did he use that expression? Didn't he talk about a girlfriend? Some girl he goes to bed with occasionally?'

'He didn't talk about her at all. The blond guy did, the one with the long hair. I think Kowalski was a little embarrassed. That's why he started talking about carrier pigeons.'

'Who is she? Where does she live? Did you find out?'

'Her name is Luisita and she has a hairdressing salon on 29th Street.'

'A hairdresser,' she said, disgusted. 'Why not a waitress?'

My joke wasn't exactly kind, but I couldn't help it. 'Maybe that's also a typical pastime of the working classes?'

But Mademoiselle didn't even hear me. 'Tomorrow I'm going to get my hair cut!'

* * *

It took some effort to persuade her that it would be me who'd have a haircut. Anyway, I told her, I was fed up with the pigtails. At school they'd be constantly pulled, and besides summer was around the corner and I'd be spending most of the day in the swimming pool. And, most importantly, I was a child. In Mademoiselle's case it was statistically proven that short hair would lessen her chances with men, as all men love women with long hair, but only one in five said they would also be happy with women with short hair. Of course I had made up these statistics on the spot.

'But I had short hair once,' Mademoiselle wondered. 'It didn't make any difference.'

Not with her, I knew that. Still, I didn't want to risk such a dramatic change at this stage. I was almost certain that a man like Kowalski would prefer women with long hair.

Even though it had become late and the hairdressing salon would no doubt be closed by now, we walked along 29th Street on the way back. We found the shop down near Whitehurst Freeway, where Georgetown wasn't nearly as rich and exclusive any more: car noise is avoided by those with expensive cars. We looked through the small shop window: it was a tiny room in a tiny stone house, which she presumably also lived in, as there were curtains on the first floor. I recognised the type from my time in Mexico. However the shop was called 'The Maharani', but as this was the only hairdressing salon on 29th Street — and the name of the proprietor was on the door — we knew that we had found the right one.

There was also a handwritten poster in the window. 'Tarot — Have your future told,' Mademoiselle read. There was a faint trace of hope in her voice. 'Carlitos, can you imagine that he's in love with someone who reads Tarot cards?'

'I don't even know what that means.' We had gone to the opposite side of the street and looked at the somewhat comical-looking house of Kowalski's Mexican hairdresser.

'A card game, where it comes from I don't

know. Very useful when it comes to conning money out of housewives and secretaries. 'My dear, the sun is next to the emperor, great fortune must be around the corner' . . . Come, we have to go home. But I'm telling you: if she has such a poster in the window, she can only be a swindler. A woman like that is capable of anything. She'd get pregnant just to force him to marry her.' She stopped in her tracks. 'Carlitos, maybe she's pregnant? Maybe that's why he calls her his fiancée?'

'But only the blond called her that.'

For a while we walked in silence in the direction of Olive Street.

'Maybe he believes in it himself,' I said.

'In what?'

'In this Tarot stuff.'

'Not Nick Kowalski,' she said. There was not a hint of doubt in her voice.

'How would you know?'

'He's a man.'

* * *

The following afternoon, right after school, we went to Luisita's hairdressing salon. It was really only a very small room, with only a single, very shabby, hairdresser's stool. Apart from the owner, there seemed to be no employees. There were also no customers.

She approached us and, like most people, stared at Mademoiselle, who was wearing her hair down that day. 'No,' she said.

'What no?' Mademoiselle laughed nervously.

'You told me on the phone you are coming for a haircut, but I won't cut that hair.'

Mademoiselle pointed at me. 'She's the customer. I'm only the nanny.'

'That's a relief,' Luisita said, but immediately realised that now I might feel insulted. 'Even though it's a shame about these wonderful pigtails.' She led me to the single chair, told me to take a seat and used the floor pedal to pump it up to children's height.

'Even Mr Kennedy likes them,' Mademoiselle said. She had sat down in an ancient wicker armchair, practically sitting in the shop window. My God, how messed up she must have been to talk such rubbish!

Luisita put a pink shawl around my neck, and a dirty towel over it. 'Which Mr Kennedy? You're not talking about the President?'

'He talked to her at a children's Christmas party.'

Luisita was suitably impressed, or at least pretended to be. 'Is that true?' And when I nodded, 'And you're sure you want to cut them off?'

'Too much work.'

'Especially with summer around the corner, right?' She held my pigtails tightly at the neck and looked at me in the mirror. 'Yes, I'm sure that short hair will suit you even better!'

* * *

Luisita Martinez was around forty, of medium height, thin and was wearing something white, which reminded me of India. What was beautiful about her was her dark mixed skin and her big, almost black eyes, which looked as if they were varnished. Not so beautiful was the permed, over-stressed black hair, which gave the impression that, due to the lack of customers, she practised on herself. But it wasn't that which made her appear a little cheap, despite the evident positive aspects of her appearance. It came from the expression of her thin-lipped mouth, the almost permanent smile, which was in evident contradiction to her hard little voice. Somehow, when you looked at her, you were reminded of a shabby dog.

'How short does the young lady want me to cut it?'

I indicated an appropriate length with my thumb and index finger.

'That short?'

I could see Mademoiselle in the mirror. She had taken a magazine, pretending to be bored, but now looked up. 'Charlotte, *est-ce que tu es certaine*?' Calling me Charlotte was no accident: the Mexican shouldn't get the idea that she could speak Spanish to me.

'*Absolument*,' I said.

Mademoiselle looked at her rival condescendingly. 'Very well, cut!'

The long-haired Luisita took a large pair of scissors and cut off my light blonde pigtails at ear height without the slightest hesitation, one cut each. 'That's it!' She put the amputated pigtails on my lap — like a cat presenting two mice it had killed to its owner, I thought. Albino mice. A moment later I thought of Stanislav and our promise. So what? Bigger things were at stake here!

Luisita asked me to lean over the washbasin.

'You want to wash my hair?' I protested.

'Do you want a good cut or not? You got to have wet hair for a good cut.'

And now, while she was washing my hair, I started the questioning as planned. Actually I was happy that I didn't have to look her in the eye. Her sharp fingernails on my scalp were punishment enough.

'The Tarot reading thing, do you do that yourself?'

She laughed. 'Don't you think I can do it?'

'I don't even know what it is.'

Evidently the subject was highly welcome. 'Tarot. My dear God, how can you explain that to a child? First of all, they're playing cards with the most beautiful paintings. From India, of course, the land of myths and miracles. But it's also something unique. Something holy, one could say. Whoever gets involved with Tarot later insists that there are two kinds of lives: one before Tarot and one after.'

'Can you use them to predict the future?'

'Depends who does it. Like everywhere, there are masters and charlatans. But with a good Tarot reader you can find out everything about yourself.'

'Also the future?'

'Only a week ago, I had a customer whose cards clearly showed a change of financial circumstances. I told her: 'Prepare for good news, Adelaida.' Two days later she calls me. Her husband had a huge pay rise!'

She bent my head back, took the towel and began to dry my hair — or what was left of it. I looked at Mademoiselle through the mirror, who was nonchalantly flicking through her magazine. 'Could you read Mademoiselle's future?'

Luisita looked at her kindly in our shared mirror. 'You know, for someone looking like your Mademoiselle, every wish will come true anyway.'

Mademoiselle laughed. Her laughter almost sounded a little hysterical to me. Perhaps it also was the disappointment that Luisita had said something so nice. The last thing she must have wanted was an endearing rival.

Luisita had now begun with the cutting and took strand after strand of my remaining hair between the index and middle finger of her left hand, and cut them with her right with breathtaking speed. Even when there was nothing to cut, she opened and closed the scissors. Presumably she thought this looked professional.

But I wasn't here to test her practical skills. 'Do you believe in miracles?' I asked.

'Do you?'

'No.'

'Well, then you won't experience one. There are no miracles for people who don't believe in them.'

'Do you think every person is surrounded by an aura?'

'I can see everyone's aura. Immediately.'

'What does mine look like?'

'I could tell you precisely.'

'Then why don't you?'

'Because that's a special thing. You don't talk about it while cutting hair.'

'Especially while cutting hair!' I said. 'Aren't you worried of cutting my aura?'

She laughed. 'I'm afraid only you could do that.'

'Like how? Through a bad deed?'

'For example.'

That was the best proof that she was lying. If I had an aura, it would be as black as my soul right now and she would have no choice but to stab me in the back with her pair of scissors.

'Suddenly so quiet? Don't you have any more questions?'

My God, we had made a complete list! I looked for help in the mirror. As if by accident, Mademoiselle now let a hand glide over her body.

'What about the astral body? Do you believe in that?'

'Why shouldn't I?' Luisita asked, amused.

'Do you think you can talk to the dead?' I asked seriously.

'But of course.'

'Can you talk to the dead?' I asked in all seriousness.

'I haven't tried it yet. But I know several people who have.'

'And what if they only wanted to show off?'

'These are all people I trust completely,' she answered.

'Do you think Jesus Christ went to heaven, and now is sitting to his father's right?'

But now Mademoiselle intervened personally. 'Charlotte!'

I always kept forgetting that she was a Catholic. Obviously the only godless person in this trio was me. I had no doubt inherited that from my mother, who defined any kind of religion as a lack of modesty: believers simply couldn't accept that something as wonderful as themselves could disappear without a trace from one day to the next. And that's also why they believe in all the other nonsense. And if someone tells them that they can talk to the dead they also believe that — after all this means that life goes on after death! That's all as far as my mother was concerned. The ideal diplomat's wife, my father occasionally remarked. Only many years later, when they were long divorced, could he smile about it. His next wife never uttered a single word about religion.

But the New Age Luisita had misunderstood everything anyway. 'Leave her,' she appeased Mademoiselle, and turned back to me: 'No, I don't believe the thing about going to heaven.'

'But there are all kinds of highly respected witnesses for it.'

She looked at me full of pity. 'Well, you

know, belief is a very personal matter. I think we should all decide for ourselves in what we believe.' I didn't yet know it then: if you start arguing with someone religious, you always end up feeling guilty. Because as soon as you have got them, they discover their tolerance and therefore yet another quality which makes them superior to the rest of us. And then they turn to someone else to preach to, since their truth can only be true when everyone believes in it.

The New Age Luisita turned around. But it was only to look for a smaller pair of scissors, as the large pair's mission seemed to have been accomplished. Mademoiselle gave me a sign in the mirror. Only then I discovered the photograph, which was hanging next to a dusty plastic tree: Nick Kowalski, no doubt.

I pointed at the picture. 'Your husband?'

She laughed. 'Well, something like that.'

'What kind of uniform is that?'

'He's with the fire department.'

'With the fire department?' I repeated, impressed.

'He's the Chief.'

'Then you can't see him very often.'

'Not during the week, both of us are too busy. But usually we spend weekends together. Saturday afternoon he goes to football, but without me . . . '

'You don't like football?'

She turned her gaze up to the ceiling. 'European football!'

'And afterwards?'

'Afterwards he picks me up and we stay together until Monday morning.'

'And what do you do?'

'You want to know everything?' She turned to Mademoiselle in mock desperation, but she had turned back to her magazine. 'His name is Nick and he breeds pigeons. Carrier pigeons. That's a lot of work. And I help him with it.' She had finished with the cutting and critically examined whether both sides were the same length. 'What's your star sign?'

'Virgo!' I said.

'I knew it . . . Well, that's it.'

I would have liked to laugh out loud. What she couldn't possibly know, she knew precisely, and about what was right under her nose, she didn't have a clue. In my opinion, the sides were of different length. But I couldn't care less.

She sprayed a gigantic portion of hair gel on her hand and rubbed the sticky mass into my hair. That must have been how she'd ruined her hair in her spare time. Then she fetched the hairdryer and brush, and began to style my new look. How fortunate that I hadn't subjected Mademoiselle to her, I thought. A hairdresser like this probably could disfigure even her.

'You're so quiet all of a sudden.'

'I'm thinking.'

'And may I ask about what?'

'Why your hairdressing salon is called 'The Maharani'.'

'Because I come from India.'

'I thought you were Mexican?'

'According to my birth certificate. We all have roots in another world, which is our real home. In my case it is India.'

'But you look like a Mexican.'

'Not to people who look with their inner eye. I was a maharani, my dear.'

'When? In a previous life?'

'Not so long ago. Go back a couple of generations and you'll have found me.'

'In India? As a maharani?'

'That's right.'

As I already mentioned, Mademoiselle's eyes always looked a little astonished. But when our gazes now met in the mirror, I saw that her mouth was open in amazement.

* * *

Later, when we were standing in the street, her eyes filled with tears. 'Carlitos, you look horrendous!'

I touched my new haircut. Two decades later punks would make this the latest fashion, but back then I was still a pioneer. 'Never mind,' I said heroically.

'She mutilated you!'

'It's much more practical this way.'

'It's unbelievable: this woman can't even cut hair!'

I pretended to be laid-back. 'At least she knows something about reading cards.'

We started to walk.

'Tell me honestly, Carlitos: what did you make of her?'

'She's an idiot.'

'You think she's stupid?'

'She'd have to read approximately one hundred books to acquire the IQ of a chimpanzee.'

'Are you just saying that to cheer me up?'

'You heard what she said.'

'Well, everyone has their belief, don't they?'

'I don't.'

We walked in the direction of M Street. As it was raining I had a good excuse to put up the hood of my raincoat. Mademoiselle simply let herself get wet.

'Don't you want to use your umbrella?'

She didn't seem to hear me. 'She has beautiful eyes.'

'They remind me of a couple of fat cockroaches.'

She laughed. 'You have comparisons!'

We had arrived on M Street, and turned left.

'But she has a good figure,' Mademoiselle insisted.

'A little too skinny.'

'No, that's not it.' She thought about it. 'Do you know what my father calls this kind of woman? *Des tissues Kleenex*.'

'Kleenex tissues?'

'You use them once and then throw them away.'

The comparison was so brutal that I spontaneously took the side of the New Age Luisita. 'I think she has nice breasts.'

'You think they're better than mine?'

Her voice sounded so tortured that I was immediately back on her side. 'Breasts! What's so important about breasts?'

Mademoiselle stopped walking. Imagine the scene: we were in M Street, the busiest street in Georgetown. As it was just before shop closing time, the pavement was full of people, and cars crawled along in the rush hour. Mademoiselle stopped walking, unbuttoned her coat and tore open her blouse, standing there with exposed breasts. Even according to my then childish standards, her breasts were sensational.

'You think that the breasts of this vulgar

little hairdresser are more beautiful than mine? Look and tell me: are you serious?'

I covered my eyes with both hands. People had stopped around us and traffic had come to a standstill. I heard them honk and howl. 'Go on, baby, do it!' someone shouted next to me from one of the cars. 'The panties!'

Finally Mademoiselle came back to her senses. It was as if she had awoken from a trance: she looked around, pulled together her blouse and took my hand. We could still hear the whistling when we turned into the next side street, walking as quickly as we could.

* * *

I think the weeks following the visit to the New Age Luisita were the most difficult for Mademoiselle. We had arrived at an impasse, and as much as we thought about it, there seemed to be no solution. Apart from one, which as far as Mademoiselle was concerned, was out of the question.

'What if we go to the fire station again?' I suggested. 'We could make up another few questions for my essay. He said that I could come to see him any time.'

'You. Not me.'

'But of course you'll be with me. That's

what my parents pay you for.'

'Carlitos, when you saw him last time, did you tell him that I was waiting for you in the cafe at the corner? Look me in the eyes: yes or no?'

'Yes.'

'You see. He's simply not interested.'

'But that's not possible.'

'And why not?'

'Because everyone is interested in you. Why, of all people, should this ugly fireman . . . '

'Carlitos!'

'OK, OK.'

* * *

The next day it continued.

'Maybe you're right,' Mademoiselle said as we were sitting down to eat.

'About what?'

'Nick Kowalski. Maybe he isn't so good-looking after all.'

I dropped my cutlery. 'Finally!'

'I'm not saying it's true. But even if it was, that's no argument. I think that especially beautiful people should choose less beautiful ones. It's all supposed to be about love, isn't it? But precisely then they're looking for their partners with a slide-rule. That's why, for example, every man tries it with me first: first the most beautiful one, he tells himself, and when she says no, I'll try one step lower. So he falls in love again and again, reduces his standards further and further and again and again breaks his heart on his way down the slope, until he finally finds someone who responds to his feelings. And why does she do that? Because she's just as good- or bad-looking as he is. Just look at couples! Neither of them is more attractive than the other: they fit as well together as if they had been picked for each other from a catalogue. If the man has a moon-face, his wife has a big nose to compensate for it. If she has short legs, he has a frail build to make up for it. This law is only broken when someone becomes rich or famous. Then he can finally get the pretty blonde he had wanted from the start. That's why everyone tries to become rich or famous, you understand?'

She took a sip of her Bordeaux. 'Carlitos, do you understand what I'm saying? I already swore to myself at your age that I wouldn't fall into this trap. Not a rich man, not a famous one, nor one of those they call good-looking. I think a beautiful person has the moral duty to choose someone less beautiful. Just like a millionaire has the duty to share his money with the poor, as a beauty millionaire you have the duty to offer yourself to someone less beautiful first. A good-looking woman who marries a good-looking man is a reactionary cow.'

'Then someone like Jackie Kennedy should have married someone like Richard Nixon.'

'*Absolument!*'

So that was Mademoiselle's 'love mathematics'. She had worked herself up into a passion — a Karl Marx of the marriage market. By the way, she spoke of her beauty without any coquetry, like someone commenting on the stock market or an incurable disease. Nor did she quote any of the hypocritical sentences other beautiful people normally use to excuse themselves: that beauty is in the eye of the beholder, every person is beautiful in one way or another, and true beauty comes from within. For the attraction that comes 'from within' we already have other names: charm, kindness, humour, intelligence. By definition 'true beauty' is always on the outside, and that makes it so unbearably unjust: there is no person who can resist it and no recipe to achieve it.

I tried one last time. 'But he's also much older!'

'So what? Should only rich old men get young beautiful women?'

'Even if he's only twelve years older than

you, you'd be his widow for twenty years.'

'Why twenty?' she asked.

'We did it in Biology. In the US men have an eight-year shorter life expectancy than women.'

'If he dies before me, I'll kill myself anyway.'

'You're not allowed to. You're a Catholic.'

'Well then, I'll think of him.'

'For twenty years?'

'I could think a hundred years about someone like Nick Kowalski without getting bored!'

She had finished eating and lit her Gauloise. After a couple of drags, she started once again: 'As far as love is concerned, Carlitos, one condition has to be fulfilled no matter what.'

'That he is a man,' I sighed.

'*Voilà*.'

⋆ ⋆ ⋆

So why was she so jealous of this hairdresser? Did her instinct tell her that Nick Kowalski, of all people, understood the matching process? That he was less blind than the other men who swarmed around her, and that this is why he didn't even try to go for someone who was so far above his level in the first place? Was he with this Luisita because he had the feeling that she was the one allocated to him according to the 'catalogue'?

On the other hand I couldn't imagine how a man of some intelligence could bear the New Age rubbish she told him. But perhaps he was just as stupid as she was, and maybe you just didn't realise it because he didn't talk much? Nick Kowalski was clearly a word-shy man and word-shy people always impress us: we just can't imagine that they have nothing to say.

'Perhaps he's just a little stupid?'

'Who?'

'Nick Kowalski. How else could he stand this ridiculous Tarot hairdresser every weekend?'

'Men are different. It's probably just like a visit to the brothel for him.'

Poor Luisita! How could Mademoiselle be so jealous of someone like her? When we were living in Rome, when I was maybe four, we had a magnificent Great Dane. A couple of months later, I got a street dog as well. My mother had hit him with her Alfa and decided to bring him home. From the day this dog arrived, the Great Dane just moaned quietly day and night. It's jealousy, my mother said, there's nothing you can do about it.

I told Mademoiselle this story.

'Et oui,' she capitulated.

But did it help?

⋆ ⋆ ⋆

Then we stopped talking about Nick Kowalski for weeks and I was beginning to think that she had forgotten about him. Other things shifted to the foreground. I finally read the three German volumes of *Winnetou* my grandparents had sent me from Vienna.

As a direct consequence, I read every book about American Indians, in whatever language I could lay my hands on. The school holidays had begun and soon it was June 11th, the day John F. Kennedy delivered his now famous speech against racism. He hadn't let himself be intimidated, and defended the rights of the blacks even more courageously than on his campaign trail. At least that's what was written in the newspapers. My parents insisted that I read one every day, including the political section.

But of course Mademoiselle hadn't forgotten Nick Kowalski. That much became clear when my mother found a New Age magazine on one of the white wicker chairs, which in the summer stood on the large terrace. She entered the library furiously, where Mademoiselle was in the process of dictating a French poem to me.

'Who is reading this garbage?'

'I bought it,' Mademoiselle said and guiltily reached for the magazine.

'You don't actually believe in this rubbish?'

That was the first time I had seen her being rude to Mademoiselle, which of course immediately put her on the defensive. 'Madame, there is hardly anyone who doesn't believe in horoscopes. At least, no woman!'

'Listen carefully, Mademoiselle,' my mother said. 'In my home in Austria and in Germany virtually all women believed in Adolf Hitler. There must have been about thirty to forty million of them. Do you think that is proof that what he preached was right?' She threw Mademoiselle's magazine back at her. 'I don't want to see anything like that in my house again. Understood?'

'Yes, madame.'

'I have forgiven you for what happened to Carlota's hair without my permission. But should I discover that you fill her almost bald head with such garbage, you'll be sitting on the next plane back to France.'

'Yes, madame.'

* * *

I tried to explain it to Mademoiselle. There were three subjects which brought my mother from nought to a hundred: old Nazis, dubbed films and, as she had just illustrated, New Age. She'd never have gone to watch a dubbed film and whenever someone asked her what star sign she was, she left them standing on the spot. 'What's your sign, dear? Which ascendant?' I swear, at least back then, she'd have stood up instantly, whoever it was who had said it.

Once, when I was older, I asked her whether she would have walked out on John F. Kennedy too. She only answered that that was the irresistible thing about Kennedy: he may have asked a woman for her telephone number, but never her ascendant. But of course, that again was a question of belief: my mother never sat next to Kennedy. The only time she saw him up close was when he said that sentence about playing with Caroline.

As far as horoscopes were concerned, she knew no excuse. Her first marriage was to a prominent German physicist who had once conducted an experiment on television that became the talk of the town. Twelve subjects, one for each star sign, were handed a horoscope in a sealed envelope, which, as they were assured, had been drawn up based on their personal data. Then everyone was escorted to an individual soundproof cabin where they opened their envelopes and read them. In the meantime, the text also appeared on the screen for the viewer. It was an elaborate, complex character analysis which only had one glitch: the text given to all twelve subjects was identical. Finally the ones who thought that the horoscope they had just read applied to them were asked to step out: of twelve participants, eleven found themselves in the duplicated horoscope, and all with absolute certainty.

I was told about that experiment many times, and of course it was explained to me why as many as eleven people believed that they had read their own personal horoscope. But it was the twelfth participant who really interested me, the one who didn't emerge from his cabin. I wanted to be like him when I grew up.

* * *

But of course Mademoiselle had only bought the New Age magazine to determine her rival's weak points. And that meant that she hadn't given up on Kowalski. I therefore asked her one more time: what if he too believed that you could get in touch with the dead? What if he thought his carrier pigeons were messengers from his Polish ancestors?

At least I had made her laugh again. 'That would be completely impossible.'

'But you hardly know him.'

'My sister Danielle joined such a crowd for a while. Actually it was more to meet a man, as she had just finished an unhappy affair. But there were no men, she said. The few who appeared at their get-togethers were more or less closet gays or genuinely messed up: they were hearing voices and having visions. And then of course there were the charlatans: Tarot card readers, fortune tellers, people who take others back to a previous life, and astrologists.'

I had an objection. 'Maybe he's gay? Maybe that's why he isn't interested in you?'

Again she had to laugh. 'Nick Kowalski isn't gay!'

'But you haven't been to bed with him? Maybe he's impotent?'

'Where did you get that word from?'

'What are your father's other rules, by the way? You said that there were another five?'

'I'll tell you some other time.'

'Do they have something to do with sex?'

She had rolled up her magazine and hit me on the head with it. 'Enough now. *Au travail!*'

But after a few minutes it was she who interrupted the lesson. 'He isn't interested in me because I'm too beautiful. He thinks he'd make a fool of himself, as he wouldn't get me anyway.'

That thought, as I already mentioned, had crossed my mind. But in this case there was nothing that could be done. 'Maybe you should get yourself a couple of scars?'

'You have ideas!'

'Maybe you should just stop washing? Or only wear ripped clothes?'

'*Allons,* Charlotte. *Au travail!*'

But the next morning, when I was sitting with my father at breakfast — my mother was a so-called night person and tended to sleep longer — Mademoiselle arrived with a gigantic bump on her forehead. My father was so shocked by the mutilation that he leapt up and pulled a chair up for her. 'My God. What on earth has happened to you?'

Mademoiselle explained she had slipped in the shower and knocked her forehead on the tap. I lowered my eyes so that she couldn't see my pity. What was she playing at with this bump? To take her adored man's fear of her beauty? And if that was the case, how did she expect to do that? Did she want to walk up and down in front of the fire station until she ran into him by chance?

How much she must love him that she

grasps at such a straw, I thought. It was time to take action.

* * *

Before I tell you about this action — it concerns, according to the strict letter of the law, a criminal act — I should tell you about the religion I had invented a couple of years previously. That was still in Lima, before Mademoiselle. One of the houses in the neighbourhood had been burgled. The old housekeeper, who Stanislav and I knew well, surprised the robbers and had to pay for it with her life.

'That happens when people no longer believe in hell,' Stanislav said. 'What should they be frightened of?'

'The police.'

'But they can't even solve one crime out of twenty.'

'You'd have to invent a new religion,' I said.

'Another one?' My friend yawned.

'One which makes belief redundant. People must know that they'll be punished.'

'Aha,' Stanislav said, with the whole superiority of her one year surplus of life experience.

'Einstein. The theory of relativity. Would you have ever thought that time stands still when you move away from earth?'

'Not stand still, you cretin. It becomes relative.'

'Alright, but a couple of years ago could you have imagined that time is such a peculiar thing? The more people explore time, I think, the greater the surprises that confront us will be. Not humbug, but completely scientific. I can imagine that the physicists of the future could find a way where everything we do today can be recalled at any time. Listen: any time. The 'now' no longer exists, as the whole time thing will be completely different to what we think today. Maybe you want to know what a certain Ricky Morales did on the 10th of October 1962 at 6 a.m. in his hotel room toilet . . . '

'I can imagine.'

'Precisely. But what if it was something completely different? Maybe he flushed the corpse of a new-born down the toilet?'

'Through the drains of a hotel toilet, right?'

'Just an example. But if he did it, only he would know.'

'And God,' Stanislav joked.

'Precisely. And he doesn't believe in him any more.'

'So he needs a new one.'

'That's precisely it: he doesn't need one. Today's religions are all so outdated, because more and more of what they used to threaten their believers with — eternal hell, eternal transmigrations of souls — becomes unsupportable from a scientific point of view. But as soon as you have to assume that an act done today can be seen by anyone at any time, you will immediately behave decently. You'd have to have a chat with a physicist. And if one day it should be possible to look at your own past, then you should tell people that today, so that they begin once again to be afraid of punishment, or at least embarrassment. Not only would the crime rate fall, but also any other kind of evil. Don't you understand? Which mother would smack her child if she knew that it would appear on her personal film?'

Of course I'm using today's vocabulary, but that's more or less the way I put it back then. But Stanislav wasn't particularly impressed and that's why we hadn't discussed my religion without belief any further. I, at least, started to fear this physical possibility, if only as some sort of superstition. Not that I behaved morally impeccably from then on, but you could say that I was more careful. Today I think that we're approaching this thing very quickly, and that's one of the reasons why I passionately follow the advances of modern physics. People already think of an eleven-dimensional cosmos, with particles without mass, probability waves and journeys even beyond the speed of light. And that's why it is also becoming less likely that the universe should be finite. Physicists like Steven Weinberg are of the opinion that in the future you may not even be able to talk about space and time any more.

But back then in Lima I had already become used to bowing in all four directions before carrying out any kind of dubious manoeuvre — even if I was only pretending to be sick before the much-despised sports lesson. Sorry everyone, I always said, and always in English. If they brought me back to the day of my misdeed, they should at least know that I was aware that whatever I was planning wasn't irreproachable. And in any case, I figured that English would be the world language by then.

* * *

I also said 'sorry, everyone' before I made my way to Mr Pilgrim with Mademoiselle on the 21st of June 1963. It had become quite hot the past few days and that's why I went out onto the terrace to bow towards the North, East, South and West. Outside, the registration of my pre-emptive admission of guilt was probably even more likely to end up on my life film. I had made a plan.

On the way to Mr Pilgrim I told Mademoiselle in every detail what he had done to me during my lessons over the past months. I did everything to make my voice sound tortured, sad and scared. And my act even worked its magic on me: I was a twelve-year-old girl who was exposed to the sexual indiscretions of a horny old teacher. It was more than understandable that I should finally confide in my nanny.

Mademoiselle had long stopped on the side-walk. 'And you only tell me about this now?'

'I didn't know . . . '

She was very upset. '*Quel cochon! Chien!* Animal! Come! We have to tell your parents immediately!'

'And then?'

'And then? This guy has to be prosecuted. He's probably doing it to other children as well!'

'And how can we prove it?'

'He will be questioned.'

'He'll say that it's a child's imagination running wild.'

'They'll question his other students.'

'They'll set dozens of child psychologists on us. Franca says Americans like nothing better than reading about that kind of thing. We'll be in the papers every day.'

‘But we have to do something! Even if you stop going, he’ll still do it to others. Maybe he’s doing even worse things!’

‘There’s only one way to prevent this.’

‘And that would be?’

‘His tool must disappear.’

‘Which tool?’ Sometimes she was really slow.

‘What’s the tool of the piano teacher?’

‘The piano,’ she said obediently.

‘An old grand piano in this case. Which stands in his pavilion.’

‘Should we blow it to . . . ’ She stopped in the middle of the sentence. ‘Carlitos!’

‘Come on,’ I said. ‘We carry on as if nothing has happened. You tell him that you want to hear me play piano just once, as our own piano hasn’t arrived yet. So today he leaves me in peace, and you can investigate the potential scene of the crime.’

‘Carlitos!’ She embraced me right there and then. ‘And it would be a highly moral affair!’

I have hardly ever been so proud, even in later life. ‘Precisely!’

* * *

Mr Pilgrim was charming to Mademoiselle. He removed a bunch of papers from his armchair and asked her to make herself comfortable. How nice that someone finally wants to listen to me play, he said, 'even if it's only the nanny'. He said it was a scandal that our grand piano hadn't arrived in Washington after so many months. I should seriously contemplate a career as a pianist, I was so amazingly talented. He instructed me to play the parts of the *Goldberg Variations* which I had already studied — she would certainly like it! There was no one who could resist the *Goldberg Variations*. Then he sat next to me on the piano bench, as usual. Only this time his hand was placed on his own leg. He never once looked at Mademoiselle. Hardly surprising, after all *little* girls were his thing. Or maybe it was just the bump on her forehead, which had turned lilac. 'Very good,' he murmured again and again. 'Very good, my child!' He had never praised me before. Now and again he took his magnifying glass to decipher parts of the score. The dedicated educationalist, no doubt about it.

And suddenly I started feeling sorry for him. I looked at his hand, covered with brown blotches, and with the long fingers of a pianist. I saw his silent trembling, which I had never noticed before. He must have wanted to become a celebrated pianist and what had become of him? A piano teacher of the children of the bourgeoisie, who had to be grateful when an unmusical employee came to listen. For I could hardly imagine that Mademoiselle was able to tell the difference between Bach and Beethoven.

Was it such a big deal when he put his hand on my thigh? Obviously he longed so much for this touch that he was willing to risk a scandal. Was I, the so-called victim, basically nothing more than a petit bourgeois skinflint? Wasn't it *my* behaviour that was perverse? For maybe a loose woman was the opposite of what everyone says: a woman who doesn't allow a man the thing he so much desires. Was the chastity of a pampered diplomat's daughter's upper thigh so much more important than the longing of a lonely old man? What was this sex everyone kept going on about? What was it apart from the longing for the greatest possible closeness to another human being?

Why was morality so complicated! Until I started to go to school, every nanny had asked me one question the first time she was alone with me. 'Who do you like best, Carlotita, Mummy or Daddy?' Every time I thought about it for a long while, and when I finally decided for one of them, I immediately thought that it was actually the other one I preferred. This was equally true with problems of morality up to this day. As soon as everyone marched in one direction — and they always marched in one direction — I had to take a look whether they hadn't forgotten something in the opposite direction. And I found that there was always something.

That's not the way you make friends. How often did I have to hear that? 'Carlota Linares — she always has to make herself interesting!' But I think that I was just searching for justice. And the longer I was looking for one answer, the more I found. Today I wouldn't even be able to define the word justice any more.

That was another reason why I admired Mademoiselle: once she had made her judgement, she never questioned it. Whether it was about Kowalski, wine connoisseurs or God — she always knew what was right and what was wrong. She could always decide, and on the spot.

She had also made her decision as far as Mr Pilgrim was concerned. Once, when I turned back to her, she gave me a sign. What? The bust of Johann Sebastian Bach? She nodded.

* * *

The bust of Johann Sebastian Bach. It wasn't made of plaster, but papier-mâché which was painted white. It was standing on the score rack, which was situated directly under the window, which around that time of year was always open. Mademoiselle thought that this was where the fire had to start. After all didn't the old pervert use this genius from Germany to touch up young girls?

Her plan was to break into the pavilion the following night, scatter the available score sheets over the grand piano, place the bust onto it, douse everything in petrol and light it with a torch thrown from a distance. I was against it.

'And why?'

'It's hardly elegant.'

'Since when does a fire have to be elegant?'

'Not the fire. The way it is lit. This will be our fourth and last fire. We should think of something special.'

'And what would be special?'

'Not a torch. We did that with the *Georgetown Queen*. And not at night. We already did it twice at night — the trash cans and the boat. I want to know what this kind of thing looks like during the day.'

Mademoiselle looked at me curiously. 'Charlotte, you're not turning into a pyromaniac, are you?'

'What's that?'

'Someone who does it for fun. *Une pyromane*.'

'For fun, for fun. We have no other choice!'

And of course Mademoiselle was highly pleased with my answer. 'Not that I can think of,' she sighed.

* * *

Already on the way home, I worked on my plan for a daylight fire with Mademoiselle. I told her that by chance I had spoken to Mr Fudimoto that morning, who regularly listened to the weather forecast on his radio: the heat would last until the weekend at least, he had said. That's also why he wanted to put off renewing the water in the swimming pool until next week. Otherwise it would have been unusable for a whole day.

'Carry on,' Mademoiselle said.

We were standing in front of the Harrimans' house, I can still remember it well. You always feel a little observed in front of important people's houses in Georgetown, and that's why I asked Mademoiselle to walk a few steps further.

'First: the bust,' I then said. 'It has to stay where it is.'

'But it's at the window. And we want to light the piano.'

'We will.'

'But not with the bust?'

'Precisely with the bust.'

'Don't make me guess, *chérie*.'

'Did you take a look at the lower part of the bust?'

'I saw the ugly copper plate it stood on, yes.'

'And what was at the edge of this copper plate?'

'His tobacco and his pipes?' she said obediently.

'Very good.' I was beginning to like the part I was playing.

'And secondly?'

'His magnifying glass. The one he uses to read his score sheets.'

'He held it in his hand,' she said.

'And at the end of the lesson? Where did he put it?'

'Next to the pipes.'

'So also on the plate.'

'I'm listening.'

'We won't start our enterprise tonight, but tomorrow night. At four o'clock in the morning, when the streets are empty.'

'But I thought you wanted a fire in the daylight?'

'I'm getting to that. We'll go there at four o'clock in the morning, but it will only be lit later that day. As he never locks the door, we don't even have to climb through the window.

Who'd steal an old grand piano, even if they could lift it? But even the window probably will be open, as he always tries to get rid of the smell of tobacco. We go there, fill the plate in which Bach's bust is standing with petrol. We pour the rest over the bust itself and a part of the curtain, which we will put over Mr Bach. And then we take Mr Pedagogue's magnifying glass, and support it over the little lake of petrol. That way, when the sun shines through it in the morning, first the petrol in the plate will ignite, then the bust, then the curtain and then the whole room, as if lit by the hands of a ghost. So old Pilgrim is punished and no one suspects a thing.'

'And what if he comes into the pavilion before it becomes hot enough? Then he'd smell the petrol? Or what if he's inside when it starts to burn? We don't want to kill him!'

'He's never at home before three in the afternoon,' I said.

'Are you sure?'

'Once I asked him whether I could come in the morning during the summer vacation. He said that he doesn't give lessons before three. Mornings he's at some kind of conservatory.'

'And why don't we do it tonight?'

'Because I'll need a day to calculate the right angle for the magnifying glass.'

We had arrived at our front door.

'Baby carriage?' Mademoiselle asked.

'School bag. This time a litre should do it.'

* * *

Everything went according to plan. Thanks to the experiments I conducted next to the swimming pool, I knew that with the angle chosen by me, the sun's focused rays would light the fire between eleven and twelve o'clock in the morning. We left an hour earlier, just in case, I with a bunch of score sheets under my arm, Mademoiselle with a shopping bag. The temperature was higher than the day before, and already at nine o'clock the thermostat read 93 degrees Fahrenheit. By ten the sun was so hot that Mademoiselle and I, changing our plans slightly, turned into the English pub on Wisconsin Avenue, from which it was only two blocks to the scene of the crime, instead of going for a stroll.

We ordered mineral water and looked out of the window, trying to appear as bored as possible. Mademoiselle had prepared for the occasion in her own way: the bump on her forehead had become a little smaller, but had taken on an even more disgusting colour. She was wearing her flowery summer dress, which the day before had looked like new. But apparently she had cut it in several places and frayed it artificially. That was the first and last time I saw a woman make herself ugly for a man.

We didn't have to wait for long. At a quarter to eleven it happened. '*Habemus Papam*,' Mademoiselle, ever the Catholic, said, discreetly pointing with her pebble-grey eyes in the direction of Mr Pilgrim's house. You could see a thin white pillar of smoke rise up into the summer sky.

Once again we had been prepared to draw attention to the fire. Under no circumstances should it be allowed to spread to the neighbouring properties. But apparently it had already been spotted, because when Mademoiselle stepped up to the bar to point out the smoke to the waiter in all innocence, the first siren started to sound. We hurried out onto the street with the other few customers and then in the direction of Mr Pilgrim's garden, from which increasingly dark smoke rose up into the sky.

* * *

A fire you light in the day isn't nearly as impressive as one you light at night. There was not a trace of blazing flames. All we could see when we approached was the gigantic black column of smoke and, in between, the outline of the small round wooden construction which had once been Mr Pilgrim's pavilion. A group of coughing people had already assembled at the garden fence, amongst them Mr Pilgrim, his hands joined behind his back, as if he had turned to stone. Apparently he had stayed at home today of all days. Was it he who had called the fire department?

And then we saw Nick Kowalski. He was standing on the first of the two fire engines — it was those I had been allowed to inspect on my visit to the fire station — and was co-ordinating his crew's fire-fighting operation using a megaphone. 'Lower the right jet. Lower. Tony, that's how you get in from the top. Yes, that's it.'

He also had discovered us. At least me. He put the megaphone aside and leant down to me. 'Hi, young lady. That must be one of yours?'

I began to laugh hysterically. 'Mine? Why mine?'

'You still needed a visual aid for your essay, admit it!'

'Sure,' I giggled.

But then he had already taken up the megaphone again. 'Not now,' he warned, and then again more energetically: 'I said not now! Can't you hear me? Step back.'

There quickly followed a loud crash. The pavilion had collapsed, apparently just what Nick Kowalski had predicted. For a few minutes you could actually see flames reaching towards the sky, but only small ones. Then it was over and the whole fire looked like no more than a gigantic barbecue.

I looked at Mademoiselle surreptitiously. After all, this had been our work, and it had turned out absolutely perfectly. But since Kowalski's arrival, she hadn't taken her eyes off her hero, who had remained calmness personified amongst all the commotion which had followed the collapse of the pavilion. 'Not so much water,' he cautioned through his megaphone. 'Bolton, turn it off. Reduce the jet, Rudi. We're not building a swimming pool.'

The whole thing took another half-hour, then he jumped off the fire engine and landed directly in front of Mademoiselle. 'What happened to you?'

She touched her bump. 'A little accident,' she laughed nervously.

'It looks like you fell among thieves.'

At that moment the tall blond came over. 'I think that's it, boss. They can manage the rest on their own.' And to Mademoiselle: 'What happened to you?'

'She slipped in the shower,' I said quickly.

'And you didn't catch her? That's what I would have done.'

That was when Mademoiselle stepped into action, not only breaking the first, but possibly all six of her father's rules: 'How about a drink, you two?' she asked, but only looking at the blond, which probably made it more acceptable to her. 'There's a pub at the corner.'

'Well, I could do with a beer,' he said, highly pleased. As he was by far the more attractive of the two, he of course thought that it was he she was interested in. 'Chief?'

'I don't know.' Nick Kowalski looked at Mademoiselle hesitantly. Was it the bump on her forehead which had finally weakened his resistance? 'Alright. But only for five minutes.'

The four of us went in the direction of the pub. Mr Pilgrim was still standing at the same spot, in the same position. A photojournalist started to work in his ash-strewn garden.

* * *

We were sitting at the same table at which Mademoiselle and I had waited for the start of the fire. Two arsonists and two firemen. It was bizarre.

When the waiter had brought the drinks — beer for the three adults, a Coke for me — we toasted each other. 'Great job,' Mademoiselle praised. And then directly to Nick Kowalski: '*Mes compliments, monsieur.*'

But he didn't let himself be duped by a little bit of French. 'How did you two get to be here again so quickly? It must be about twenty minutes from Olive Street?'

'I have piano lessons with Mr Pilgrim,' I said and showed him sheet music as if it was proof. 'I had piano lessons,' I giggled.

'What a coincidence, again,' Kowalski smiled mysteriously. I don't think that he already had suspicions back then — only my bad conscience must have made it seem that way. When my father came home late and my mother — sometimes certainly in all innocence — asked for the reason, he always asked her why she had to be so suspicious. I really wouldn't like to see my father's film!

But also I continued as if I had just been accused. 'We were too early and that's why we waited here. And then Mademoiselle spotted the smoke.'

'*Habemus Papam*,' she repeated her modest joke. When Kowalski didn't seem to understand her, she explained: 'That's what they say when they've elected a new pope.

That's when they let white smoke rise up into the sky. That's the way it looked. At the beginning, I mean.'

'No one ever told me about that,' Kowalski said. 'What a shame. And my parents are Catholics.'

'Mine too!' Mademoiselle shouted, as if this was the most amazing coincidence in the world. 'What I miss here in America, is soccer.' She had said it so suddenly that I feared the worst.

But Kowalski seemed highly pleased. 'You like soccer?'

'Sure!'

'I wouldn't have expected that from you.'

'First it was my father. I could hardly walk when he dragged me along to matches. But later it got to me worse than him.'

'Well, my thing is baseball,' said the blond, whose name was Frank by the way, and who wanted to get back into the ring. 'I'll take you any time.'

'I don't know anything about baseball.'

'I'll teach you.'

'Football,' Mademoiselle insisted.

'That would be the Chief's thing,' the blond Frank capitulated. You could see that he couldn't get it into his head that Mademoiselle wouldn't prefer to go with him, no matter what game. And basically I felt the same way.

Of course now there was no escape for Kowalski. 'I go to a soccer match every Saturday,' he said. 'Maybe it's the European side of my family. Do you two want to come along one of these days?' You two. He didn't want to be alone with her.

'Are you serious?' Mademoiselle beamed nevertheless.

'Of course it's not like in France,' he tried to discourage her. 'SC Washington versus SC Boston, SC Washington versus SC Baltimore. Small soccer grounds. And usually the guests win. You must be used to better.'

'You know, they're not that good in Biarritz either. Biarritz is a tiny town.'

Kowalski tried one last evasive manoeuvre. 'But the young lady will be bored.'

But he really had picked the wrong person. 'In Buenos Aires I always used to go to the River Plate games with my grandfather. He's been their sponsor for a thousand years or so.'

'All experts,' Kowalski capitulated. He had finished his beer and stood up. 'Thank you.'

'Well, see you Saturday,' Mademoiselle said quickly. 'When and where?'

'I almost forgot.' He took a pad out of his pocket and in energetic letters wrote down the time and place of their first rendezvous. And then he added his private telephone number, just in case something came up. For us, not him. Nothing ever interfered with his soccer.

* * *

I knew that there was no way Mademoiselle could be a soccer fan. I had already known her for half a year and couldn't recall her having used the word football a single time. What I didn't know was that she hadn't even seen a single match in her life. A waste of time and money, her apparently so-called football-crazy father used to say. Men should go and see a good strip show instead.

'Not even on TV?' I asked her.

'What?'

'You haven't even seen a football match on television?'

'I tried once. *C'était l'ennui total*.'

'So how are you planning to get away with it? I mean, he'll know, won't he?'

'We have another four days to Saturday. I'll be perfect by then.'

'At football?!'

'*Mais oui*.'

'And how are you planning to do that?'

'You will teach me.'

* * *

Amongst the toys in the basement was an old table football game. We took it up, dusted it and put it under the parasol next to the swimming pool. Some of the footballers lined up on the poles were damaged, but at least Mademoiselle knew that a team consisted of eleven men.

'Plus goalkeeper,' she said proudly.

'Already included.'

'Ah.'

Luckily there was an instruction leaflet with the game, listing all football rules. Using these teaching aids, we systematically concerned ourselves with the matter at hand over the next four days. The lessons started at nine o'clock in the morning and took most of the day. Before dinner I had scheduled an hour-long examination:

'What's a free kick?'

'A free kick is the continuation of the game after the opposing team breaks the rules. The opposing team members have to be at least 9.15 metres from the ball.'

'And in American measurements?'

'As I studied my football in France, I would have no idea.'

'Correct. What's a foul?'

'A deliberate breaking of the rules in fighting for the ball.'

'A centre pass?'

‘A far and high ball, which is hit from the edge of the field towards the goal.’

‘Very good!’ I was obviously the born teacher. ‘And what is a penalty kick?’

‘A penalty kick is the continuation of play after a foul in the penalty area.’

‘And where is it taken from?’

‘Eleven metres from the centre of the goal.’

‘What’s called ‘out’?’

‘Outside the playing area.’

‘What’s called defensive?’

She took a deep breath. ‘A defensive team is out to secure their own goal and operate out of a stronger defence.’

‘Very good.’ I was really impressed.

‘You really think so?’

‘By Saturday you will know more than I do.’

‘Keep asking questions!’

And I did: about low passes, centre forwards, sending-off, red cards, yellow cards . . . It was absolutely fascinating how quickly she could grasp something she was completely indifferent to. I can only understand things that interest me.

Mademoiselle only showed genuine interest as far as the matter of own goals was concerned. ‘There really is such a thing?’

‘I’ve seen it with my own eyes.’

‘My God, the poor player. I’d kill myself if

something like that happened to me.'

'My grandfather knew someone who did. The following night he went out onto the pitch and hanged himself on the goalpost, where he had shot the own goal.'

'An Argentinian?'

'Who else? Whenever our national team comes home after a lost away match they have to be put under police protection.'

'Because the fans would kill them?'

'Sure.' For a moment I felt like an Argentinian. That wonderful country, all those crazy people! I'd ask my parents to let me live with my grandparents in Buenos Aires. Or with my gay Uncle Sergio, the builder. They'd hardly miss me; they never saw me anyway. But then came the next question and the feeling had passed.

Then the famous Saturday arrived. Mademoiselle had changed a dozen times and finally decided, at my suggestion, on jeans with a blouse cut like a man's shirt. On no account should she look more attractive than she usually did. The bump on her head had shrunk to a red brown dot. It looked nasty, but you'd only know if you stepped right up to her.

The small football ground, the name of which I can no longer remember, and which was mainly frequented by South Americans and Europeans, was situated a little outside town. My father had insisted that Leopold drove us, and he was instructed to wait for us in the car park. Should Kowalski invite Mademoiselle for something after the match, I would say goodbye and be driven home alone.

He was waiting for us at the arranged spot. He had a friend with him, who he apparently always went to football with: a well-built black man with a half-greying beard. A colleague, Kowalski said, stationed in Foggy Bottom, the district where he lived. He called him Adair and also explained why. There wasn't a fire he didn't know what to do with. Just like the real Adair. Mademoiselle and I nodded knowingly, but we had heard neither of the fake nor the real Adair. As I found out later, the real Adair, first name Red, was *the* American fireman. Whenever there was a really difficult fire, Red Adair would be flown in and he'd always find a solution. Of course the fake Adair was also immediately captivated by Mademoiselle. The bump on her forehead didn't seem to bother him in the slightest.

Kowalski had organised the tickets and we had good seats. We sat down, Mademoiselle and I between the men, and we could arrange it so that Mademoiselle came to sit next to Kowalski. The men explained to us the peculiarities of the two teams: the match was against SC Brooklyn and of course they were hoping for a victory for SC Washington, even though they had never won against this team before.

* * *

Then the match began. We had discussed at length how Mademoiselle should behave. In any case, she shouldn't show too much excitement, which would only reveal the newcomer. Here and there, when the home team got into a dangerous situation, a small outcry was allowed, but to be on the safe side always a moment after the others. And it goes without saying that 'our' team had to be Kowalski's. That much I had learned from my Argentinian grandfather. No man would be able to bear it if someone next to him screamed for the opposite team. If your own team scored, you were of course allowed to scream to your heart's content.

Everything went without hitch, at least until half-time. My lessons evidently had been extraordinarily effective. When Mademoiselle showed an emotion, it was always restrained, and came at the right place and at the right time. Occasionally she asked Kowalski about a particular player, who had just excelled himself. But as time went on, she became more and more frivolous. Seemingly unintentionally, she kept her denim-covered legs apart, so that her right thigh touched Kowalski's. I had to think of Mr Pilgrim — he'd have been arrested for such behaviour. Once — it was almost the end of the first half — my heart almost stopped when she clearly shouted foul, and before everyone else. But it really was a foul: half a second after her scream, the referee took out a yellow card, and a young boy, who was sitting in front of us, turned to look at her full of admiration.

Then came half-time and Mademoiselle left to get ice cream for us all. The men talked about a fire that had devastated a skyscraper in Chicago the previous day. It sounded quite frightening and I asked the fake Adair why firemen weren't afraid when faced with such situations. Just the opposite, he said, you're always afraid. He was in Korea for a year, but compared to a major fire, that was 'peanuts'. I realised that he was talking about a fire as if it were human. 'It's his tricks, kid, understand? He always plays with you. He can crawl through the tiniest hole, suddenly leap up a couple of floors. He passes through a window as if it didn't exist, and if he wants to he can manage an elevator shaft in seconds without leaving a trace!'

I liked him, the fake Adair. And for a couple of moments I even liked Kowalski — maybe only because he picked someone like him to go to football matches with. You can't go with just anyone to a football match, my grandfather had always said. But I was convinced that he would have gone to football with the fake Adair.

* * *

But then, after half-time, disaster struck. The ball landed in the goal and Mademoiselle threw herself around Kowalski jubilantly.

He gently pushed her away and said: 'That was a goal for the other team.'

'But why? The ball was in the net!'

'That's right. But here the teams have the strange habit of switching sides at half-time.'

I wanted to disappear into the ground! Of course it had all been my fault: I had told her everything under the sun, but I had forgotten to inform her that teams change sides after half-time!

I don't know how Kowalski explained this lapse to himself. Maybe he just thought that

Mademoiselle knew it was a goal for the other team, and only pretended to make a mistake to have an excuse to fall around his neck? For even he must have realised by now that she was after him — neither Adair nor I seemed to exist for her.

But somehow it all worked out nevertheless. Maybe her embrace had been less uncomfortable for him than I had assumed? On the other hand it might have had something to do with the way the match turned out. During the remaining thirty minutes, SC Washington managed, against all expectations, to score two goals. Of course she didn't fall around his neck this time. When the game was over, he and his friend were highly satisfied. Adair even said that this game would make history.

'That's us!' Mademoiselle said. 'We bring luck, don't we, Carlitos?'

'Then we'll need you Saturday in two weeks. It's SC Boston's turn and we haven't scored against them since 1952.' It was Kowalski who had said it. Unbelievable!

Mademoiselle asked whether she could invite him and his friend for a drink. After all he had bought the tickets. But he said that was OK, and that unfortunately he had made other arrangements. Adair, so invincible as far as fires were concerned, was obviously too shy to cope with Mademoiselle's beauty on his own.

* * *

Two weeks of pure happiness followed — at least as far as Mademoiselle was concerned, I hasten to add, because for me the whole thing was quite exhausting. To be honest, I would have preferred to light another fire than to see Mademoiselle in this condition. Because of the chauffeur, she had pretended to be comparatively nonchalant on the way back from the football ground, but as soon as we had arrived back home it all erupted: 'He wants to see me again! He wants to see me again, Carlitos, did you hear what he said? I bring him luck!'

'We bring him luck,' I corrected her. 'He wants to see us again!'

'But he only said that not to make it too easy for me. Not that I think that he doesn't like you. Someone who doesn't like you must be an idiot. But you're a child. It was me he was really talking about.'

Very well. After all, it was she who had experience with men, not me. And besides, I really couldn't care less whether this boring fireman wanted to see me again.

'Of course you'll have to come. Otherwise

he'll think that I'm after him.'

My God, if he hadn't realised that by now, he really was a little slow!

'Rule number one. Remember?' she said.

I did.

* * *

And that's how it continued for a whole week: 'Did you see the way he looked at me when I fell around his neck by mistake? When the other team scored a goal? I'm not saying that he's already in love with me. But he definitely has caught fire!' She was so amused by the comparison that she had to repeat it a couple of times. 'A fireman who catches fire, isn't that funny?'

She sent a whole flood of postcards to her friends in Biarritz, and each one said in one way or another how beautiful America was. And the men! What luck that they couldn't see Kowalski face to face. They'd get a dozen yawn attacks each.

One evening, I surprised her at the pool. She was dangling her perfect legs in the water and was holding her French matchbox in her hand, one by one striking matches: '*Il m'aime . . . Il ne m'aime pas*.' The match always lit when she said 'He loves me', and she threw it into the pool, laughing happily. When she said

'He loves me not' she used so little force that the match had no chance of lighting in the first place. Those matches she threw behind her with complete disgust. Once one of the 'He loves me not' matches started to burn after a small delay, and lit a dry leaf in the little bamboo forest behind Mademoiselle. Even though I was barefoot, I immediately jumped on it to put it out: a fifth fire was the last thing we needed.

Mademoiselle turned to me. 'Carlitos, what are you doing in the bushes? I thought you were sleeping?'

* * *

Around the middle of that week, she suddenly had the wish to walk past Mr Pilgrim's house to see what had happened at the site of the fire. But all traces had already been removed and where the pavilion once had stood, there was an immaculately cleaned grey spot. Only the slightly sooty wall of Mr Pilgrim's house was a reminder of the catastrophe.

'That was quick,' Mademoiselle said. She sounded almost disappointed.

I, on the other hand, was relieved. 'Maybe he was well insured. He'll construct a new pavilion as quickly as possible. If it's a prefab, it'll be up in a week.'

'So it will start all over again? No, that guy won't get away with it so easily! Compared to the others, that fire was a just one, don't you forget!'

'But I won't go there any more anyhow. I think I'd rather take violin lessons.'

'Violin lessons?'

'I think it'd be about a thousand times more interesting.'

'Violin lessons! My youngest sister takes violin lessons. When she practises, everyone walks around with plugs in their ears.'

'Well, I'd like it.'

'Very well. Maybe I'm just not musical. Just like him. Country and Western! That's what he said, didn't he?' She smiled happily.

Even so, I couldn't talk her out of giving Mr Pilgrim an additional warning. Our deed shouldn't have been in vain, she insisted. I would have to think of the other students.

'Maybe he only did it with me? Once he said that I was the only one who at least had an idea what music is all about.'

'And that's why he touched you up? Because you can play the piano so well? *Mais comme tu es naïve!*'

At home we formulated three sentences. Mademoiselle put on her elegant black leather gloves and typed them on a clean sheet on my father's typewriter. YOU DIRTY OLD PIG. THE FIRE WAS A WARNING. THE NEXT TIME WE'LL SHOP YOU TO THE POLICE.

'If he only did it with me, he now knows who the arsonists were.' I asked her to consider.

'He didn't only do it with you. And even if he did, he won't report us.'

She wrote Mr Pilgrim's address on an envelope, enclosed the sheet and put a stamp on it. I offered to mail the letter immediately and even walked the few hundred metres to the nearest letterbox. But there I tore it into a thousand pieces, which on the way home I threw at intervals onto the pavement, just like in the Hansel and Gretel fairy tale. However, in this case, I didn't bow: to decide who was wrong and who was right I would have had to look at Mr Pilgrim's personal film. (Today I see this differently of course: this had been a hugely problematic weakness as far as he was concerned.)

When I came back, Mademoiselle was still sitting at the typewriter, but without gloves. 'Come here,' she said. She had written down her future name, in two versions. On one sheet was the French version: Madame Catherine Kowalski. The other sheet contained the American one: Mrs Nikolas Kowalski.

'Which one do you prefer?'

I pretended to throw up. 'Never!'

'Never what?'

'I would never take the name of a man. Not even under torture.'

Mademoiselle smiled forgivingly. 'We'll see.'

* * *

Practically every day that fortnight, I had to stroll past the New Age Luisita's hairdressing salon with Mademoiselle, where the poster with the offer of Tarot readings amused her again and again. '*Pauvre imbécile!*'

Once her rival stood at the door in person, right next to the poster and once again dressed up as an Indian. When she gave us a friendly wave, I brushed over my messed-up haircut appreciatively.

'Great!' I shouted over to her.

'Thanks!' she shouted back. No hint of self-criticism. You would have thought that she'd won the first prize in a competition of the Washington hairdressers' union.

'In a way I feel sorry for her,' Mademoiselle said.

'You feel sorry for her?'

'Well, he will leave her. But actually that's the best thing that could happen to her.'

'Why?'

She sighed. 'He's a Catholic, you heard yourself.'

'His parents are Catholic,' I corrected her.

'Same thing, you can never get your religion out of your system. And she's definitely hooked on New Age. Basically she needs someone who believes in the astral body.'

'But you said there aren't any men like that?'

'Some moron will turn up sooner or later.'

* * *

Pride comes before a fall, my Austrian grandmother always used to say — and some people fall so quickly that they think they're flying. Here the fall was also inevitable. And, my God, from what height!

When the long-awaited Saturday finally came, Mademoiselle threw caution to the wind as she was so sure that she had won, and made mistake after mistake. In football terms you would say that she used all her talents to shoot not only one own goal, but several.

It started with her choice of clothes. Instead of sticking with the tried and tested jeans, this time she picked a dress! A red dress! While it was tailored quite conservatively and wasn't too low-cut, her magnificent back was only covered by two thin crossed straps and the skirt was so short and tight that none of her sensational curves were left to the imagination.

Her skin had become bronze through the time spent by the pool, which made her pebble-grey eyes glow even brighter. She was wearing no make-up — why should she? — and of course the bump on her forehead had also disappeared. In short, Mademoiselle was more beautiful than ever and this time she didn't only know it, she wanted it that way.

'Mistake,' I said as she walked up and down in front of me before it was time to go.

'What's a mistake?'

'Everything. You said yourself that he may be frightened by your beauty.'

'*Tempi passati!*' she laughed, full of high spirits. 'In the meantime, Monsieur caught fire and I will pour oil on that fire. It has to blaze!'

* * *

Leopold once again chauffeured us to the football ground. My parents had left for a summer vacation in the Hamptons, where they had rented a cottage at the beach with two other couples. Of course I should have gone too, but in that case they would also have had to invite Mademoiselle. Whoever had seen her in a bikini could imagine what damage she could inflict on three married couples in two weeks, and so they were quite content to leave me in her care in Washington. Apart from that, my parents also knew that I didn't care much for beach vacations. You are constantly full of sand and covered in mosquito bites.

This time we arrived before Nick Kowalski, and exactly what I had feared and Mademoiselle had calculated happened: a circle of male admirers formed around us, apparently in no hurry to get into the ground. They must have been curious about the man who was lucky enough to go to a football match with a creature like her. When Kowalski finally arrived and it became apparent that it was him she had been waiting for — she welcomed him with a kiss on each cheek — he was greeted with several ironic comments. To add to the misfortune, not even the fake Adair, who might have been able to save the situation, was there. He had been ordered south to attend to forest fires in Florida.

So we entered the football ground, just the

three of us, where Mademoiselle was greeted with whistles by everyone she walked past. But she still didn't understand what was going on, and even went so far as to take Kowalski's arm. A man wants to be proud of the woman who accompanies him, she thought.

We sat down, Mademoiselle first, and then Kowalski pushed me energetically into the row so that I came to be seated between them, as some sort of buffer. Still she wouldn't understand a thing, as she now began to flirt with him above my head without a hint of restraint. She asked him about his work, his pigeons. She said that she had thought of him several times this past week.

'Why?' he asked in a tone of voice which I immediately recognised as cold, but she obviously thought was very macho.

'No idea,' she laughed. 'Just like that.'

* * *

SC Washington played abominably. At the end of the first half, the opposing team had scored five goals and Kowalski's team hadn't managed a single one. Mademoiselle had misjudged several of her shouts — and probably thought that it wasn't that important anyway. When half-time came, I said I had to go to the toilet urgently and it was vital that Mademoiselle came with me. She got up unwillingly and followed me.

'Are you crazy?' she hissed when we were out of earshot.

'I have to talk to you!' I hissed back. But when we finally found the toilet it was so full that I dragged her out again. And there was Nick Kowalski, waiting for us.

I can still remember the scene as if it were yesterday: to the right the wall of the ladies' toilets, painted in pink, to the left the gents', in sky blue. In between, Nick Kowalski, who had lit a cigarette. It was the first time I had seen him smoke. He offered the packet to Mademoiselle, but she refused.

'I have to talk to you,' he said seriously.

Mademoiselle looked from him to me, amused: 'Is this a conspiracy?' When I shook my head, she turned back to him: 'Right here? Between the toilets?'

He laughed nervously. 'As good a place as any. And it won't take long.'

I wanted to get out of there as quickly as possible, but he grabbed my elbow. 'Stay. I don't have the impression that you two keep secrets from each other.'

Mademoiselle now lit one of her own cigarettes: Gauloises and matches, obviously she kept them handy all the time. 'Well?' She blew the smoke in his direction, as if she wanted to caress him with it. She was probably expecting a proposal of marriage or something of that nature.

'I don't know,' Kowalski began hesitantly. 'I could be wrong, you know? In which case I'll have to beg your forgiveness. Basically, what I'm about to say sounds absurd. I mean, considering your looks and all that. There probably isn't a single guy in the football ground you couldn't have.'

'I don't believe it,' Mademoiselle smiled. 'The Chief is paying me a compliment!'

'That was not my intention,' he replied, now completely calm. 'I would even say that it's probably more the opposite. But as I said, I could be mistaken. But I have the impression . . . '

'You have the impression . . . ?'

'I have the impression you're after me.'

I had anticipated a put-down, but not such a brutal one. Mademoiselle wasn't anticipating anything. She just stood there and stared at him.

'And if that was the case . . . As I said I can't be sure, why should it be me of all people . . . '

'When I could have the entire football ground,' Mademoiselle added. 'Including the two teams, no?' Her voice sounded neither ironic nor hurt. Without inflection would be the right description.

'Right. I think that you're playing some kind of game with me. Maybe you've made a stupid bet with each other? That would also explain why you know so little about football. I'm talking about you, not the young lady.' He looked at me and then again at Mademoiselle. And now came a reply from Mademoiselle he hadn't expected.

'I love you,' she said. She said it with such simplicity, such seriousness, that Kowalski was lost for words.

I had closed my eyes as if I could stop all this from happening, but now I looked up at her: Mademoiselle was standing very upright and looked him directly in the eye. I have never admired someone as much as this beautiful French woman, who had been stabbed through the heart standing between two toilets at an American soccer ground.

Finally Kowalski was able to speak again. 'You love me?' he asked.

'Since Christmas, yes. When you came to Olive Street for the first time. The Christmas tree. Remember?'

There was another pause.

'Well,' Kowalski said. 'I don't love you.'

Mademoiselle laughed bravely. 'Because you can't love someone like me?'

'I didn't say that.'

'Because there is someone else?'

There was another pause. 'Yes.'

Mademoiselle extinguished her cigarette with her foot. Only now I realised that she was also wearing her high-heeled shoes. 'May I ask who the lucky one is? Is it this New Age hairdresser?'

It took a moment until he had orientated himself: 'Yes.'

'And you love her.' It was fact, not a question and she didn't say it condescendingly. Thank God.

'Love, love . . . Who knows what love is? It's a five-year-long stable relationship. You can't just go after the first . . . ' He realised that he had said something wrong and shrugged his shoulders. 'She helps me with the pigeons.'

'Of course,' Mademoiselle said. She moved behind me and put her arms around me. It was as if she wanted to hold on to me. I felt her shaking like a leaf.

And suddenly I became more angry than I had ever been before. I tore myself away from Mademoiselle, leapt towards Kowalski and began to hit him with both fists.

'Carlitos!' Mademoiselle shouted and tried to pull me away from him. 'Carlitos, stop!'

But I only hit him harder and now also

started to scream: 'You idiot! You pathetic little fireman! Have you ever looked in the mirror, you bald nobody? How dare you . . . How dare you . . . '

It would have been easy for Kowalski to stop me. One movement of his hand would have sufficed. But he just let me beat him without lifting a finger. And maybe that was what finally made me come back to my senses. In any case I turned away and pushed my face against the rough plaster of the light-blue toilet wall, where I now started to sob as unashamedly as I had beaten him. Kowalski stepped up to me and put his big hand on my spiky hair. 'It's OK, kid,' he said softly. 'It's OK now.'

Mademoiselle touched my shoulder gently. 'Come now, Carlitos . . . Come, let's get back to the car.'

I don't know whether she looked back at him, my eyes were blinded by tears. That's probably also why she now took me by the hand and led me through the assembled bystanders down to the exit. Behind us a whistle announced the second half.

Mademoiselle's journey through hell had taken all but fifteen minutes.

* * *

For a while we drove silently.

'*Eh bien*,' Mademoiselle finally said. 'Mr Nikolas Kowalski. *Fin de ce chapitre*.'

'Over and out,' I added. And when she didn't say anything in response, I added: 'Pilots' lingo.'

'Well, maybe next time I should choose a pilot. You only need one short sentence at the end.'

I tried to imitate Kowalski's accent. 'I could be wrong, you know . . . There probably isn't a single guy in the football ground you couldn't have.'

I had hoped to make her laugh with my impression, but she only raised the screen between the driver and us. 'You know what? They always say that the one who is dumped is the loser. But, I ask myself, is that really true? The fact is that I loved him and he didn't love me. At least I had a feeling, and what a feeling it was! And what did he have?'

'Not a thing.'

'Exactly. Therefore he's the one who should be pitied. Who's the loser?'

'He is,' I said.

'*C'est ça*,' Mademoiselle said. And after a while, she added: 'I remember when our teacher asked what we would prefer: to love or to be loved. The whole class, including the boys, decided that they preferred to be loved.

I was the only one who preferred to love.'

That wasn't a surprise. All the boys were probably in love with her anyway. Not even the spotty Kim Fulder was in love with me, and he was really the last choice.

Again we were quiet for a long while. 'My God, I hope he'll be happy with his little hairdresser!' she suddenly shouted.

'His shabby doggie!' I don't know why I suddenly felt like laughing, but I just started to anyway.

'With his shabby doggie, yes!' Strangely enough she also started to laugh. 'If only she wasn't so vulgar. I really thought he'd have better taste. Do you know what she looks like to me?'

'Like a shabby doggie?' I was still laughing.

'No. For me she looks the way a petite bourgeoise thinks a femme fatale looks. And after all, he's a petit bourgeois. He breeds pigeons on his roof terrace. What is it today? Saturday? I'm sure that's where they'll be sitting tonight, searching the sky for UFOs.'

'And, if they find one, they send a pigeon to meet it. A carrier pigeon carrying a letter in its mouth.'

'In its beak,' Mademoiselle giggled. 'Pigeons have beaks.'

'Hello, you extra-terrestrials! We're two astral bodies, ready for our journey through the universe! . . . And if they don't come to get them, you know what they will do?'

'What?'

'They'll fly together to India because the Maharani needs a new sari for her wedding night.'

'Wrong,' said Mademoiselle. 'New Agers don't have wedding nights. They transform their sexual energy into a spiritual one.'

'You mean they don't go to bed together?'

'A little tantra, perhaps. But once a month at the most. She helps him with the pigeons, you heard it yourself!' She was shaking with laughter.

* * *

I only described the conversation in the car in so much detail as I wanted to show how little I could have been prepared for what happened that night. Somehow I thought: well, it must have come as a shock for her, but now she's once and for all cured of this guy. As quickly as she had fallen into this passion, she had fallen out of it.

I was the only one whose bedroom looked out to the front. At some point that night I heard somebody open a garage door — by hand. We were the only ones in that area who had to open their garage doors manually

— my father never stopped complaining about this injustice — so I knew immediately that it must be our garage, and crawled out of bed and walked over to the window. I saw Mademoiselle step out of the garage into the moonlight and cross the street. She was carrying something in her right hand, which was obviously heavy: a canister, filled with petrol, no doubt. In her left hand she carried a longish object, probably a jack. I ran out of the room as I was, in pyjamas. When I got to the front door, she had already disappeared from sight. But of course I knew where she was heading.

As soon as I turned into 29th Street, she reappeared no more than twenty metres in front of me. She was walking neither fast nor slow, and never turned to look back. She walked as if it was the middle of the day and she was on her way to get a baguette for her employers.

Why didn't I stop her? Why didn't I try to bring her back to her senses? Because I knew that I wouldn't have succeeded? Or because I didn't want her to get back to her senses in the first place? And if not, why? Had I already identified with her that much that I too felt the urge to punish the New Age Luisita? Punish her for what? This reincarnated Mexican from India had no clue that she was in Mademoiselle's way. After all Kowalski wasn't a gossip, so she wouldn't have the slightest idea of Mademoiselle's obsession!

Or was I just hungry for the fire itself that night? Had our four fires made me long for more? Of course I would have interfered if I had thought that there would be a living thing in Luisita's house. But if she had a pet, it would have been in the salon on the day of my haircut. To me, she looked like someone who'd even take a parrot to bed. And of course she herself would be safe, as she spent every Saturday night with Kowalski. No, if Mademoiselle had to do what she had to do, it was the perfect moment. I hurried up my steps: in the meantime my enthusiasm had grown so much that I even forgot to bow for my film.

Mademoiselle had arrived at her unsuspecting rival's house. Without once looking right or left, she approached the glass door and smashed it with the jack, right next to the door handle. No one seemed to have heard the shattering of the glass; the surrounding houses remained dark. As if she had done nothing else all her life, Mademoiselle put her hand through the hole and opened the shop door from inside. Then she took the petrol canister and entered. I saw her tear off the hated Tarot poster and throw it out into the street. Then she disappeared inside the hairdresser's. Presumably she distributed the petrol carefully over the carpeted floor, just as we had rehearsed for the burning of the boat. For that she would have to start in the back room.

She had left the jack carelessly at the entrance, and I crossed the street to retrieve it, as I was sure she would forget. Then I returned to the opposite side of the street and waited. It didn't take more than three minutes for her to reappear — without the canister of course. I saw her searching for something in the pockets of her jeans.

My God, she can't have forgotten her matches? I thought. Now of all times? But of course she hadn't forgotten them. Who leaves home to burn a house down and forgets to take matches? She lit one and threw it through the open door into the petrol-doused room. I thought I'd have to pull her away from there, but as the flames started to flare up, she came to the opposite side of the street of her own accord. Not because she was afraid, I sensed, but because she would have a better view from there. She wanted to see it burn! She still hadn't noticed me.

It didn't take more than a couple of minutes for the New Age Luisita's shop to be ablaze. We both stood there without moving, not even five metres apart from each other. Neither of us could avert our glance from the increasingly furious fire. Only when the window panes started to burst with a loud crash did I walk over to her.

'Mademoiselle!' I called quietly.

She turned to me. 'Carlitos?' she asked politely. 'What are you doing here?'

A light went on in one of the neighbouring houses.

But she only had eyes for her work. '*C'est tellement plus beau la nuit, n'est-ce pas?*'

'We have to get out of here!'

'But no, we should enjoy it, Charlotte. After all, it's our last.'

'But he won't come. It's Saturday! He's never on duty Saturdays!'

'You think I started this fire for the fat little Polack? It's only for my own pleasure!' She laughed happily.

'Then let's go! Everyone can see us, in this moonlight!'

The first siren sounded in the distance. I pulled her by the hand.

'Mademoiselle, please! They're coming!'

The first fire engine had already pulled into 29th Street, when I finally succeeded in dragging her to the footpath. From there she followed me unwillingly in the direction of

Olive Street, again and again looking back at her fire.

* * *

This time the newspapers reported the fire at length. They wrote that the incidents of unexplained fires had increased substantially in our neighbourhood. First there was the fire on the *Georgetown Queen*, without doubt arson with petrol, as the spectroscopic analysis had shown. Then there was the fire at the piano teacher's house, the cause of which couldn't yet be established, but which presumably also was the result of a criminal action. And now the fire that devastated a hairdressing salon on 29th Street, whose owner, interestingly enough, was the fiancee of the local fire chief. Even the trash cans lit back in the spring were worthy of mention. Yet it was impossible to find a common denominator for the fires, let alone a motive. But as practically the entire political elite resided in Georgetown, political reasons could not be ruled out. However, it was more likely that the fires were the work of one or several pyromaniacs. Neighbours had seen a woman and a boy of approximately ten years at the site of the last fire. Harmless spectators, presumably, who were politely requested to make themselves known to the police. Every little piece of information was important.

I showed the article, which was illustrated with several pictures, to Mademoiselle, who only shrugged her shoulders. I shouldn't worry, she said. If they should ever find us, she'd take all the blame. After all it was all her fault.

But they didn't find us. For a few days I got a fright whenever someone rang the doorbell. But then my parents returned from their holidays, suntanned and overloaded with presents. They had brought a football for Mademoiselle, as they had thought her sudden interest in the sport was genuine. When she promptly started to cry, they took her tears for tears of joy. So as not to disappoint them, she went out onto the terrace to kick the ball around the garden. She did it with such anger that it went as far as past the bamboo forest. My parents applauded. When I went to look for it, I found it floating in the pool. I fished it out and hid it in the changing house, so she'd never have to see it again.

Otherwise there had been a change within Mademoiselle. Instead of making fun of Kowalski as in the beginning of what I had mistaken as being the start of her recovery process, she now started to worship him again. She was the one to be blamed for his rejection. If she had acted a little more sensibly, she would have won him. That red dress! Why hadn't I warned her?

'But I did.'

'Not enough!'

She had dressed herself like a whore! And how could she have been so stupid as to confess her love to him? 'How did you get the idea I could be interested in you?' That would have been the right answer! What was left to conquer in a woman who told a man 'I love you'?

That I assured her how much I admired her, especially for that, and that it was the only great thing about the whole rotten episode, didn't help one iota. In one of the thousand coffee-table books that were lying around the house, she had discovered a picture of a painting by Titian. It was entitled *Noli me tangere* and depicted Jesus of Nazareth with the sinner Mary Magdalene. He looked down at her condescendingly, holding a white sheet against his soft body with the big stomach. She was on her knees next to him, obviously consumed by passion.

'There, you see it? That's how I approached him! That's how I adored him! I can't believe it!'

'That's not true,' I said. 'This Christ is just someone who stood model for this Titian guy. And he wouldn't have liked Mary Magdalene, or Marilyn Monroe for that matter. He's gay.'

She tore the book out of my hands. 'What do you know about gays? A mere child!' But when she had studied the reproduction one more time, she handed the volume back to me without a word.

Of course I didn't know the first thing about gays. I had only ever met one in my life and that was Uncle Sergio, whom I have already mentioned, my father's older brother, who ran a construction firm in Buenos Aires. He hadn't even admitted it to himself: an Argentinian man is no homosexual, especially not one who spends his entire day on building sites. His fear that someone should think of him as being gay went so far that he didn't have a single male friend — he wouldn't even have gone for a bite to eat with another man, my mother claimed. His language was spiked with sexual innuendo, so that you should get the impression that he was only thinking about one thing. And he always told everyone that he kept three lovers. There used to be five, but that had become too much even for a man like him. Then there were the constant phone calls from his women, who seemed to be driven to the edge of madness by jealousy, because of course he had also told them that they would have to share him with rivals: after all he was a man who loved the truth. After a while, it became evident that he didn't do much with any of his so-called lovers. He probably only arranged this story of the triangle so that every woman thought he was too exhausted due to his orgies with the other two, that he didn't have any more in him for her. And of course she then felt like dirt. This game only ended when he met a sexy lesbian who even had a child, and was playing the same charade he was. He married her shortly before his fiftieth birthday. When she became pregnant — apparently he occasionally did it after all — one of his deserted lovers was so overcome by a deep depression that she climbed onto the roof of one of his apartment blocks in the middle of Buenos Aires, and jumped to her death. For him, his disguise was now even more perfect: women killed themselves because of him!

And this Jesus of Nazareth painted by Titian looked exactly like this Uncle Sergio from Buenos Aires. I had a weakness for my sadistic uncle, by the way. Or maybe only for his dog — the best-educated crossbreed you could imagine, and so devoted to his master that he even lay next to him at his drawing board. I always thought that the dog was the only creature this uncle, punished with the wrong genes, dared to love. For that reason I felt infinite pity for him. If society forces a man who preferred to love men to perform such a farce, is he to blame or the others? I thought the solution with the lesbian was nothing less than a stroke of genius. By the way, the whole family pretended to fall for his act. The only people who didn't know that everyone knew were the uncle and his so-called wife. For me they were the saddest couple in the world.

But of course this story didn't cheer up Mademoiselle either. A few days later I found her dress of shame in the rubbish. It was in rags, to be safe, so no one could retrieve it and parade it in front of her, the uniform of her private Waterloo.

⋆ ⋆ ⋆

Her jealousy of the New Age Luisita became more grotesque by the day. She probably hadn't had reason to be jealous of another woman in her entire life — after all, men usually tried her first — and that's presumably why it now hit her with increased ferocity. Presumably her whole love-mathematics theory went down the drain: a man who was neither famous, rich nor good-looking preferred a woman whom no one else would have noticed in Mademoiselle's presence. That's how John F. Kennedy must have felt when, in 1961, the Russians were first in space with Yuri Gagarin. That's probably why he demanded billions of dollars from the American Congress for his own space adventure. Brotherhood was neither here nor there: the richest and most powerful nation on Earth had to be first to land on the moon. Only if they hadn't been interested in this satellite could the rival have it. But, as chance would have it, the United States was interested in this moon.

Not a day passed when Mademoiselle didn't dial Kowalski's private number and every time the other woman answered. The first time she still spoke, without even trying to hide her distinctive French accent. 'Could I speak to Nick please?' And then: 'Thank you very much, I'll try again later.'

She banged the receiver back on its cradle. 'She lives with him! Can you believe it, Carlitos? The whore has actually moved in with him!'

'What else could she have done? You burnt her house down.'

'Right,' mumbled Mademoiselle. After a while she added: 'Own goal.'

And for a while at least I was afraid that

one morning I would find her hanging from one of the ashen beams of Luisita's former hairdressing salon.

* * *

But then she became calmer. Too calm, as I realise today, but back then I was grateful. Kowalski wasn't mentioned any more, and once in a while she even went out with other men. Even the playboy surgeon got another chance, though I can't imagine he got very far. When he had driven her home in his BMW from some restaurant, she would lean against the inside front door after he had gone, as if she had just finished a spell of hard labour.

Once I heard her tell my mother that she had seen Kennedy.

'Which one? Jack?'

'The other one, the Attorney General.'

'Bobby. And well, did he talk to you?'

She laughed: 'It was at church.'

'In the Catholic church?'

'Apparently he's a Catholic.'

'All Kennedys are Catholics,' my mother said impatiently. 'I'm just surprised that he didn't talk to you.'

I'm aware that this conversation sounds absurd. But Mademoiselle's beauty was so enormous that it seemed inconceivable that the Attorney General of the most powerful nation in the world wouldn't disturb her at her prayers.

* * *

She apparently had begun to attend church regularly. Of course I couldn't help asking her why.

'Because I love God,' she answered simply.

'More than Nick Kowalski?'

'That's over.'

'And why do you love God?'

Evidently she remembered her duty as a missionary: 'There are many reasons. For example, because he had his only son crucified.'

'Despite,' I corrected her.

'What do you mean?'

'You should say: despite the fact he had his only son crucified. Otherwise people could think you're a sadist.'

She looked at me, her pebble-grey eyes full of leniency. I still dared to say such things back then, but in the meantime I have become too afraid of hurting my opponent. Yet no one ever seemed to wonder whether they were hurting me. When they insisted that they could communicate with the dead, for example. Or that you are born into a different body when you die. Or that you are miserable in this life because you have committed horrific crimes in a previous one.

'Is that also true for children who have been abused?' I once, much later, asked a self-confessed Buddhist. 'How about the sick? And those who are starving to death right now?'

'As horrible as this may sound, madam, that's the truth.'

'And the Jews in the concentration camps?'

'Of course. How else could you explain their suffering? Where would the sense be?'

Back then, no one seemed to ask themselves whether they might make a fool of themselves in front of me, the child. More and more I felt as if I was in a gigantic zoo: in one cage those believing in resurrection and going to heaven, in the other those into reincarnation on Earth, in the next one those who are waiting for the appearance of the Messiah, in yet another, the ones with auras and astral bodies and the destiny which is written in horoscopes. In between was me, the crazy little zoo assistant, feeding each species with her awkward questions, which earned the inevitable nonsensical, but always kind, answers.

'It was only a question,' I now quickly said to Mademoiselle to prevent the worst. There are people you don't contradict because you like them too much, and others because you have too little respect for them. As far as Mademoiselle was concerned, it was clearly a consideration of the first variation. I think I really liked her.

* * *

As well as going to church regularly, Mademoiselle was beginning to talk more and more about France. At one of the rare dinners we had with my parents, she told them that she was thinking of going back home. After all, it had been almost a year.

'But not immediately, I hope?' my father asked. No, no, there was no hurry, she only wanted to prepare us for it. I tried to look at her eyes across the table, but she avoided my glance. My mother asked her to stay at least until the beginning of December. They would be in Argentina in November, where I couldn't accompany them because of school. And Mademoiselle was the only one they trusted to take care of me.

✾

'I say to you today, my friends, that in spite of the difficulties and frustrations of the moment, I still have a dream. It is a dream deeply rooted in the American dream. I have a dream that one day this nation will rise up and live out the true meaning of its creed: 'We hold these truths to be self-evident: that all men are created equal.' I have a dream that one day on the red hills of Georgia the sons of former slaves and the sons of former slave owners will be able to sit down together at the table of brotherhood. I have a dream . . . '

That's how Martin Luther King started his historic speech which he delivered on the 28th of August 1963 at Washington's Lincoln Memorial in front of a quarter of a million mostly black civil rights activists. John F. Kennedy wasn't present but he had cancelled all appointments so he could listen to it on the radio. My mother and I also listened to it on the radio, and both of us were in tears.

Afterwards I asked her why you had to cry listening to a speech like that: because you know that now everything will be different or because you know that nothing will change anyway? Of course my mother didn't have an answer. She only knew that back at home people also started to cry when they were listening to Adolf Hitler's outpourings.

Nevertheless, I decided that this speech should, at least for me, have personal consequences. Should someone put up the dividing screen between us whites conversing in the back of the limo and our black driver, I would ask him to stop and sit in the front with him.

Oddly enough, the very next day there was a good reason for putting my decision into practice. As usual I was sitting between my parents when they began to fight. Apparently my father had started having an affair with a young embassy employee and my mother had found out. For my benefit the conflict was at first coded and restrained, until they forgot about me as usual and became more and more explicit. And that was precisely the moment when my father put up the dividing screen.

He then immediately became defensive. 'You married an Argentinian man! You should have known we're different from your European sissies!'

'Oh yes? Like how? I only know two Argentinian men, you and your brother. One is a skirt-chaser who pretends to be a faithful husband, the other a homosexual who pretends to be a skirt-chaser!'

Should I have sat in front with Leopold at that of all moments? I knew that he couldn't understand Spanish, and so wouldn't be missing much, unlike me.

* * *

In the meantime it had turned September and school had started again. On the first day I handed in my essay on Nick Kowalski to Mrs Cook. It was almost twenty pages long and was still entitled 'My Hero', but now with an added question mark. I asked Mademoiselle whether she wanted to read it, but she pretended not to be interested in the slightest.

Maybe she would even have enjoyed the essay, the state she was in. As usual I had put the whole thing on its head: I followed a long introduction with a song of praise for the men of the fire department — with special consideration of Nick Kowalski — and for this profession which, in my opinion, was the last one where someone could still prove his courage. Then I asked who — apart from accidents and negligence — he had to thank for this opportunity to prove his courage. Well, arsonists of course!

Without arsonists, no fire department, without evil no good. The rest of the essay concerned the contributions criminals made to society. I started to list the number of jobs that we owe to those who make their living or satisfy their lust by cheating, blackmailing, robbing, raping, torturing, murdering or maiming the law-abiding amongst us. Jobs with the police, with insurance companies, emergency wards, in physical and psychological rehabilitation centres, in detective agencies, in lawyers' offices, in the judicial authorities, forensic medicine, prisons, locksmiths and alarm-system manufacturers and so on. And as the success of a criminal act lies in its unpredictability, I wrote that these were also some of the most varied and interesting of jobs. It was unthinkable what would happen if, from one day to the next, we all became kind, honest people, full of integrity. As people fighting criminals are usually 'doers', the consequences of their sudden unemployment would be psychologically devastating. And you shouldn't forget that the entertainment industry is also profiting from the criminals. For how do we relax in our spare time? What are the television programmes and films we like to see most about? What are newspapers, novels and plays about? About the conflict between good and evil and therefore crime, am I right?

And so it went on. I don't want to reproduce the entire essay here, this is only by way of explanation of how the sixth fire came to be. But first back to Mrs Cook. It didn't take more than three days until she took me aside after the English lesson to talk about my 'thesis'. At first she didn't know what she should make of it — but now she was completely enthusiastic. She had also given it to Mr Brown, the headmaster, to read and he had the idea that I should read it out to parents and students at the annual assembly. Because my ideas were so daring, it would be a good opportunity to show the parents that one tried to promote originality and unconventional thought at Georgetown Day School.

The usually so blasé Mrs Cook was completely ecstatic, and was probably even convinced that you could really learn original thinking. In my opinion, someone either dares to think or not, and luckily this has hardly anything to do with education. If it had, all diplomats would be original thinkers and all taxi drivers idiotic conformists. Usually I get the impression that exactly the opposite is true.

But of course I didn't tell her that. To be honest, I have to admit that for the first time I found Mrs Cook sympathetic. It is quite difficult to think of someone who has just described you as a great thinker as an idiot. I therefore told her what she expected from me: 'many thanks', 'unbelievable honour' and so on, and how proud my parents would be.

'And they have every reason to be!' my benefactor said with a victorious smile. I was already halfway out the door when she called after me to tell me that she had invited this fireman. It would be interesting to see what he would make of my opinions.

'You invited Nick Kowalski?'

'You don't have to be frightened of him. I will defend you like a lion!'

'He accepted?'

'He seems to be a nice man. If his duties allow him, he'll be at your talk.'

* * *

Mademoiselle was waiting for me at the bus stop as usual. During the trip I had decided not to tell her about this thing. But we hadn't even turned into Olive Street when I came out with it.

'Are you going to come?' I asked after I had told her.

'No.'

'If you don't come, he'll think that you're afraid. And why are you afraid? Because you're still in love with him.'

'That's true, I still love him. But I won't come.'

* * *

However, when I was driving with my parents to the reception at our school on the first

Friday evening in October, Mademoiselle was sitting with us in the car. As the temperature was once again wintry, she was wearing the grey woollen costume she had arrived in at Washington airport almost precisely a year earlier. And like then she had tied back her dark blonde hair firmly. And not a trace of make-up. Under no circumstances should he think that she had made herself pretty for him.

Mr Brown stood at the entrance and greeted the parents with handshakes and the students with casual comments. To me he said: 'Ah, our star!' Yet it was a while until I was able to shine with my masterpiece. First there were drinks, followed by a speech by the headmaster along with the presentation of the new teachers. Even then, there was still Mrs Cook's introduction to live through, which mainly consisted of a string of pre-emptive apologies. One had thought long and hard about whether to impose such unorthodox and probably underdeveloped thoughts on the parents. What a chicken!

Before she finally handed over the podium to me, she casually mentioned that she had invited the portrayed fireman, a Mr Nick Kowalski, to participate in the discussion which was to follow. But he had just let her know that because of tightened regulations

— one must have heard of the recent spate of arson attacks in Georgetown — he couldn't be with us. She had hardly finished when Mademoiselle stood up and left the assembly room. If it had been anyone else no one would have noticed, but as it was Mademoiselle everyone looked at her. It would have been futile to start reading the essay before she had shut the door behind her.

But then I began with the lecture. It was, as it were, my first public appearance, but after a few mistakes and a few friendly calls from the audience asking me to speak up, I quickly got going. I had been reading for maybe ten minutes and just finished the introduction, when, believe it or not, I just said: 'And now to the fire department . . . ' when an excited voice could be heard shouting, 'Fire! Fire!'

Of course my audience first started to laugh, as they thought of this as nothing more than a student prank. But then Herb Dearfield, a boy from my class, stormed in and shouted once again, 'Fire!' As the laughter became even more lively, he stormed onto the podium: 'For fuck's sake, this is no joke! There's a fire out there.'

Now everyone tried to leave the festively decorated hall at the same time. Not because they thought they were in mortal danger — Georgetown Day School was a somewhat modest building and we were on the ground floor — but because everyone wanted to see the fire. It actually was worth seeing. Not because of its size or its danger, but because of the unusual arrangement. It had started in the grey garden house — more of a shed actually — which stood right in the middle of our school yard, and was used to house not only all the sports equipment, but also the school's waste paper, which was bundled and ready to be taken away. Someone must have filled the door-opening with some paper and lit it, presumably with matches and without any inflammable addition — if petrol had been used, according to my experience, the whole garden house would have already stood in flames. The whole thing looked more cosy than dangerous — because of the careful arrangement between the prettily painted door posts, the whole thing looked more like a well-supervised chimney fire. In any case it was quickly brought under control. Before the fire department turned up, the director and the janitor had buried the whole thing under thick foam.

Of course no one wanted to return to the lecture after this adventure, not even my parents. When the fire department had left we walked back to our car, where Mademoiselle, sitting in the back, was leafing through one of my mother's fashion magazines.

'What a pity,' my father said. 'I'll read your oeuvre tonight, I promise!'

'All that for nothing,' my mother complained. 'If it had at least been a real fire!' She turned to me: 'Do you have any idea who may have started it?'

'Someone in her class who begrudged her performance,' my father said.

'Maybe even the one who shouted,' I added. 'Herb Dearfield, this idiot. He handed in an essay about his grandmother's health care worker. Unbelievable achievement.'

The next day, a personal letter from the director was delivered by courier in which he assured parents how much he regretted this incident and that he would find the person responsible. If the culprit was found amongst the students, it would have the harshest consequences. But of course the culprit wasn't found amongst the students. I knew perfectly well that Mademoiselle had lit the fire. Her sixth, as I said. I didn't even have to ask her why she had lit it. She wanted to prove her power to Nick Kowalski. She wanted to show him that his cancellation was no use. If she wanted to, she could conjure him up at any time of night or day. She really couldn't have known that the Georgetown Day School lay just beyond the borders of

Georgetown and therefore came under the jurisdiction of another fire station.

* * *

It was ten days later when Mademoiselle collected me from the school bus and kissed me on each cheek that a car stopped next to us. In this car, an old Chevrolet, sat none other than Nick Kowalski. He wound down the window and asked us to get in.

'You want us to do what?' Mademoiselle said unbelievingly.

'I would like to ask you to get into the car for a moment. I have to talk to you.'

'Again?' Mademoiselle said with all the spite she was able to muster, considering her surprise.

'It won't take long.' When I wanted to slip away discreetly, he added: 'That goes for you too, young lady.'

'I have to do my homework.'

'That can wait.'

So we got into the back of his car. I let myself sink into the shabby seats with a theatrical sigh, as if the whole thing was very inconvenient for me. I hadn't seen such a run-down car for ages, maybe ever. Kowalski started the engine and slowly let the car roll into Olive Street. Was he planning to take us home?

He stopped the car a few metres before our house and turned to us. 'I have thought about this for a long time. Added one thing to another, or maybe better added one to five. It always adds up to you two.'

'Maybe you could explain,' Mademoiselle said coolly.

'That's what I'm here for. The unsolved fires. I can think of five at which you've been present. And had the opportunity to light. The other fires in Georgetown this year have all been solved.'

'I'm afraid I don't follow, monsieur.'

'You understand me perfectly well.'

'Which fires are you talking about?'

'Not the one at Christmas. That must have been an accident. But this one . . . ' Only now I realised that he had stopped right in front of the three trash cans, which of course in the meantime had been replaced by brand-new ones. 'This was arson and of course both of you were on the spot immediately. Then came the unexplained fire on the boat. I wasn't on duty, but I enquired whether you might have been amongst the spectators. And you, Mademoiselle, are not easy to miss.'

'Thank you.'

'Then there was the old piano teacher's pavilion, who by coincidence you visited at that hour. I called him: he never gives lessons in the morning, no exceptions.'

'Carry on.'

'Now to the fire which personally interests me most. The hairdresser's. A woman was seen at the scene. A woman and a boy.' He looked at me. 'But that could also have been a girl with short hair, am I right? Oddly enough, that happened the night after our last conversation. When, amongst other things, we talked of my relationship with a certain hairdresser.'

'The New Age Luisita,' I said.

'The New Age Luisita,' he repeated kindly. Then he turned to Mademoiselle again: 'She tells me that a few months ago you were at her salon with the young lady. She remembered you, as you're not the kind of clients she usually has.'

'Do you believe in horoscopes?' I asked quickly.

He laughed. 'In horoscopes? No.'

'Why not?'

'If everything's written in the stars, there's nothing for us to decide any more. Over with freedom, correct?'

'Correct.' My God, how my mother would have liked this answer!

But he didn't let himself be side-tracked. 'Afterwards, you constantly walked past her shop. And, she says that since she has moved in with me, there are these constant phone calls. Once there was a woman with a French accent. And there aren't many of those around here.'

'Continue,' Mademoiselle said.

'And now to the fire in the school, which also remains unsolved. A harmless fire but still: you never know how something like that can spread. Especially when the arsonists are amateurs.'

There was a long pause.

'Why don't you go to the police?' Mademoiselle finally asked. 'Isn't that your duty?'

'I first wanted to know what you make of the whole thing.'

'Well, what should I make of it? I think all of these fires were extremely . . . ' She looked at me questioningly: '*Réussis?*'

'Successful.'

'But maybe that's just my vanity,' Mademoiselle said. 'After all I started them all.'

He now looked at me: 'Together with the young lady.'

'Carlota had nothing to do with it.'

'*She* had nothing to do with it!' I yelled indignantly. 'She wouldn't have had enough technical knowledge to think about stuff like that.'

'You used a magnifying glass with the teacher?'

'Right,' I said.

He raised his thumb in acknowledgement. 'Good work.'

Now Mademoiselle went back on the offensive, this time very energetically: 'She's making it up! Maybe she gave me some advice here or there. But the inspiration always came from me.'

'Are you a pyromaniac?'

Mademoiselle had to laugh. '*Une pyromane? Mais non!*'

'What does that mean?'

'That means no, I'm not a pyromaniac.'

'But why then?'

'That is my problem.'

'You burn half of Georgetown and you don't even want to give me, the fire chief, a reason? I'll tell you one thing: that is just not possible.'

Mademoiselle thought about it for a while. 'Of course there was a reason.'

'For God's sake, tell me!'

'I wanted to see you again.'

'You wanted to what?'

'I wanted to see you again.'

This time the pause seemed to take an eternity. Nick Kowalski turned back to stare through his Chevy's dirty windscreen. 'You seriously want me to believe that you have laid all these fires because you hoped I would turn up?' He was still not looking at her.

'That's the way it is.'

'That cannot be true.'

'But it is true, *voilà*!' She looked out of the side window as if the whole conversation didn't concern her.

'I mean you of all people, who could . . . '

'Could have anyone. You repeat yourself, monsieur.'

He turned back to her with a desperate laugh: 'But there are thousands of other possibilities, if you want to see a man. You don't have to burn a house down every time!'

'For example?'

'For example,' Kowalski repeated in a voice which almost sounded desperate. 'You could have walked into my office any day and invited me for a cup of coffee.'

'That just wasn't possible.'

'And why not?'

'You remember the way it was at the football ground? You said you had the feeling I was running after you. The first step has to come from the man, that's a golden rule!'

'And if this man happens to be with the fire department, you just have to light a fire. That's how he gets the opportunity to make that first step.'

'*C'est ça*,' Mademoiselle said.

'What does that mean?'

'That means that's the way it is.'

'So it is. And now?'

'Well, you want to know whether I'm planning to start more fires? Don't worry about it, I am going back.'

'To France?' Was it my imagination or was there a brief moment of shock?

'That's where I come from.'

'When?'

'Soon.'

There was a pause. Kowalski looked at Mademoiselle with a strange expression. 'I'm sorry,' he said. 'I mean I'm sorry that I disappointed you so much.'

'As you can see, I survived it. Is the interrogation finished? May we leave?'

'Of course.' He got out of the car, but before he was able to walk to the other side to open the door for Mademoiselle, she was already standing on the sidewalk. He could only help yours truly to get out of his luxurious limo.

'Well then . . . ' He offered Mademoiselle his hand, however she took mine that same moment.

'All the best,' she said with a distant smile and we walked the few steps to the door of the house. When I turned back, Kowalski was still standing next to his car.

* * *

'You were careless,' Mademoiselle said, when we entered the house.

'I was careless?'

'You shouldn't have told him that you were a part of it.'

'But it's the truth.'

'The truth, the truth! What if he goes to the police?'

'He won't.'

'It's his duty. If he stays silent, he incriminates himself. It could cost him his job.'

'He still won't do it.'

'What makes you so sure?'

This time it was I who said it. 'Because someone like Nick Kowalski knows what to do. He's a man.'

My parents flew to Argentina at the end of October. While my mother packed the suitcases I sat on the so-called marital bed and read her an article from *Newsweek*. According to opinion polls, John F. Kennedy had already lost four and a half per cent of the white vote due to his championing of civil rights; in the South neither the whites nor the blacks liked him. The whites didn't vote for him because he wanted to help the blacks get their rights, and the blacks because they thought it happened too slowly. Of course Martin Luther King's march on Washington and his speech at the Lincoln Memorial had only made things worse.

'Darling, I'm sorry to interrupt you,' my mother said. 'Have you seen my sleeping pills? I know that I had a full tube. It's just disappeared.'

'Maybe Daddy took them?'

'Impossible. He sleeps like a stone.'

'Would there have been enough to kill yourself?'

'Twice over.'

As soon as they had left the house, and my mother had waved back a hundred times as usual — she always had a bad conscience when she left me alone for a long time, still she never stayed — I sneaked into Mademoiselle's basement apartment. She wasn't at home because she had to run some errands. As expected, I found the tube of pills. In the middle of the table — she hadn't even bothered to hide it.

I took it, ran upstairs and found a tube of calcium pills in my parents' medicine cabinet, which were of the same colour and size. I swapped them with the sleeping pills, apart from two, which I replaced on top. Who knows, maybe she only stole the tablets because she couldn't sleep, which wouldn't have surprised me. And if she was out to kill herself, two tablets wouldn't be enough. I took the tube back down and put it where I had found it.

* * *

I don't know why she waited until the 18th of November. Maybe it was because of my parents, whose trip she didn't want to ruin too early on. Maybe she wasn't even sure whether Kowalski was worth dying for. And even though her God had long been replaced by this fireman, she may well have had some religious reservations. When she didn't appear for breakfast on the 19th of November — normally she came down much earlier and helped me prepare for school — I immediately knew what had happened. I sneaked into the garden, from which you could see into her small bedroom. She lay on her pink-covered bed, a real sleeping beauty. On the bedside table lay the presumably empty tube of pills and an envelope, which presumably contained her suicide note.

I walked around the house to the front and rang at her door. After what seemed like an eternity she opened the door in her night-gown, completely confused, but alive! I congratulated myself on the idea of leaving the two real sleeping tablets. As she had actually fallen into a deep sleep after she had taken them, she'd probably assume that the pills simply weren't strong enough. If she hadn't fallen asleep, she might have tried it another way and now it would be too late.

I fired explanations at her: 'I've got another stomach ache. I can't go to school. I'm not making it up, I swear! Would you be so kind . . . I mean, would you . . . ?' As she still seemed completely absent, I tried it in French. '*Mademoiselle, est-ce que vous auriez la gentillesse de téléphoner à mon école?*'

'*A ton école? Mais pourquoi?*'

'*Parce que je suis malade!*' I put my hands on my stomach, looking miserable.

'*Mais oui, ma chérie. Attends, j'arrive tout de suite!*'

* * *

Ten minutes later she was sitting in the drawing room, freshly showered, looking at a magnificent bunch of flowers an admirer had sent the day before. It must be a strange feeling, I thought, to have said goodbye to everything and then you're suddenly still there. Just as if you were embarking on a journey around the world, and missed the train. But on this occasion it was me who had to play the part of the sufferer.

'Do you want me to call a doctor?' Mademoiselle asked.

'Not necessary. They're just the usual stomach cramps. I'll be better soon.'

'Are you sure?' She looked so worried that I almost had to laugh. She had counted on lying in some mortuary by this time, and now she wanted to call a doctor because of my little stomach pain. I just wanted to sleep a little, I said. Here, on the sofa.

She pointed towards the garden, where Mr Fudimoto was sawing up the rotten tree which he had felled the day before. 'You won't get any sleep with this noise. Wouldn't you prefer to go to bed?'

But I only shook my head weakly and closed my eyes. When she then sneaked on tiptoe to Franca in the kitchen, I began behind my closed eyelids to make plans for the seventh and positively last fire. Not that I was expecting any great miracles from it: it should be a small, modest fire, just concocted to distract Mademoiselle from her intention for the next few hours or days. After that I would think of something.

And this should also be my fire alone. But, in a strange way, this also became one of

Mademoiselle's fires. Or, to put it a better way, into a fire for the three of us. After all it would also determine Nick Kowalski's destiny.

⋆ ⋆ ⋆

It was the sound of Mr Fudimoto's chainsaw which gave me the idea. I knew that it would be interrupted at exactly noon, and taken up again at exactly two o'clock, as Mr Fudimoto was an extremely punctual and conscientious man. I also knew that he would lock his precious chainsaw into the changing house during the lunch break. That's precisely where he found me when he returned, smoking one of Mademoiselle's Gauloises. I begged him not to tell on me. He shook his head disapprovingly, and climbed back down into the pool with his saw to continue his work. That was the first part of my plan taken care of.

The second part proved a little more difficult. I had planned to pour a generous portion of petrol over Mr Fudimoto's cut-up wood and let a cigarette fall on it as if by accident. This would have produced a highly visible fire, but one which was strictly limited to the basin of the empty pool, where no one and nothing would come to harm. Just a little clearing-up work, which I would of course volunteer for and a new lick of paint for the pool, which anyway was long overdue. I would do that too, on my own, to prove my readiness for repentance. After the incident with the cigarette the conscientious Mr Fudimoto would certainly report that he saw the daughter of the house secretly smoking the French nanny's cigarettes.

But when I came to get the petrol from the garage, I realised that both cars were missing. My mother's Alfa had been taken for a check-up and Leopold had apparently taken out my father's Mercedes. I had to find another solution. Because of the general hysteria that was caused by the unsolved fires, it would be impossible just to go and buy a couple of litres of petrol at the local gas station. But of course I found another solution. In the basement workshop there was, amongst the numerous pots of paint, a huge, untouched tin of paint thinner. On it the longed-for warning: 'Do not expose to fire! Danger of explosion!'

Danger of explosion was exactly what was called for. I went back to the pool with a tin of sky-blue paint, a couple of paintbrushes and, of course, the paint thinner, and asked Mr Fudimoto what time he would finish work that day. Exactly at five — of course I knew that already. I told him I wanted to try a certain sky blue at the edge of the pool. The pool would have to be repainted in the spring anyway. Again he shook his head full of disapproval. That meant that he would later be able to recollect my undertaking.

When he left through the garden gate at five o'clock precisely, I stepped into action. He had put the wood he had cut into a high, round stack, approximately one metre in diameter. Quite an achievement, and an unnecessary one at that, as the wood would later be kept under the terrace. But that's what the Japanese are like, Franca used to say. Everything had to be aesthetically pleasing, you could already tell from their food. As Mr Fudimoto had covered the swimming pool floor with thick newspapers to avoid scratches, a lot of paper was at my disposal. I put some of it in between the stacked pieces of wood, and added whatever I could find of shavings and the spirit tablets Mademoiselle had already used with the rubbish containers. I crowned the stack with the tin of paint thinner, which I surrounded with a thick ring of rolled-up newspapers, and which was glowing like a golden crown in the evening sun. Then I sneaked back into the drawing room and again played sick.

As was arranged whenever my parents

weren't home, as there wasn't much to cook, Franca also left the house, at seven o'clock precisely. The cleaning women and maids only came in the morning anyway. In other words: now Mademoiselle and I were alone. We sat at the table in the breakfast room, where Franca had prepared a cold meal for us. Now I only had to deliver a great performance. And most importantly, I shouldn't eat a thing.

'You're not eating,' Mademoiselle remarked as I had expected. 'Do you want me to make you some soup?'

'No, please don't, I couldn't eat a spoonful,' I told her. 'My stomach pain is even worse now than in the morning.' I asked her to get a certain kind of pill from the medicine cabinet, which had always helped me in such circumstances. She found the packet immediately, and of course I had made sure that it would be empty. Of course she now offered to take my bicycle and cycle to the drugstore on M Street. I thanked her, playing the suffering child perfectly. That would give me the twenty minutes I needed.

As soon as she had closed the front door behind her, I slipped into my anorak and ran over to the swimming pool. I lit the wooden stack with the same technique I usually used to start the fire in the fireplace in the drawing room. As the material was prepared perfectly, it started to burn quickly and with some ferocity. I congratulated myself on the idea of doing it all in the protected place of the empty pool. It was a somewhat windy evening and, without shelter, the lighting of a fire on such a scale would no doubt have proved difficult. In any case the flames were soon so high that despite the bamboo forest, which covered the view to the pool from the house, it could be seen from there. High time, therefore, to call the fire department.

I stood alone in the drawing room, looking in the direction of the fire, receiver in my hand, the duty officer of the fire department on the other end. And then it happened. Danger of explosion — I had read it on the can, but didn't really count on what I now experienced: a bang so loud that even the guy on the other end of the telephone heard it. Everywhere burning debris flew through the air.

'Hello, hello . . . ' the duty officer shouted. 'Are you still there?'

'Yes.'

'What happened?'

'Something exploded!' I screamed.

'I heard that. Hello?'

'Yes.'

'Calm, stay calm. How old are you?'

'It's burning! There are flames everywhere!'

'The address!' He also had started to scream.

'The bamboo forest. It's burning like crazy! . . . The fire is coming towards the house!'

'Tell me your address! Can you hear me?'

'Yes.'

'You have to tell me where you live!'

I told him. 'Nick Kowalski has to come!' Now I was really in panic. 'Nick Kowalski has to come, quickly.'

As I said this, the fire was already engulfing the terrace.

* * *

Maybe it was because of the wind that everything went so quickly. The wind as well as the bamboo forest, which was completely dried out as, despite the time of year, it hadn't rained much. Stupidly I had left the terrace door open when I had made the call, as it was supposed to look real and spontaneous. But now, as I tried to escape through the front door out into the street, a draught sucked in the flames when I opened it. They looked like a bunch of frivolous guests you had invited for a drink.

But at least now I was outside. The streets were deserted as always. Even though the first windows started to crack on the ground floor, no one had noticed the catastrophe yet. I should have yelled 'Fire!' as my mother did last Christmas, but for some reason I didn't think of it. Maybe it wouldn't have been much use anyway — I had the impression that in this street of the rich and world-travelled, no one was home anyway. While it wasn't quite dark yet, it was not light enough so you wouldn't need lights inside, and no lights were on in any of the neighbouring houses.

Sometimes I still think that I didn't shout for help because I enjoyed the whole thing too much. I was standing on the opposite side of the street and looking at our house, which was burning more and more magnificently. The flames were in the process of conquering the middle floor, and I could feel the heat on my side of the street. Then I heard the quiet rattling sound, which at that time used to accompany the television reports about Vietnam. If the fire department didn't arrive immediately, nothing would remain, that much was certain.

And the sky! I had seen fires at day, fires at night, but none at sunset. With each minute, it became more impressive. Not just because of the flames, but because of the smoke, which emerged from our house more and more thickly and in all imaginable colours: blue, lilac, yellow, ochre and, of course, all shades of grey. Behind it lay Washington's evening sky, furnished by the friendly director of my spectacle with all varieties of pink. Some people are just lucky.

Lucky! I bowed quickly for my film, and of course I knew that this fire — of course never planned on this scale — wasn't a heroic deed. But I only bowed in the direction of the burning house, so I wouldn't miss one second of this misdeed that had gone so out of control.

In addition to all this, I felt an unbelievable feeling of freedom, which was probably the reason that I now started to giggle like a madwoman. It is a different feeling watching a building burn in which nothing belongs to you than the house which contains everything you own. In the meantime everything that my parents considered worth owning and showing off had arrived from Lima, and had been put in the designated places. That's probably the best way to find out whether you are one of those people who are attached to material things or one of those, a much rarer kind, who couldn't care less. As it now transpired, I was clearly one of the latter. That became even more apparent when the window of my room now exploded with a loud bang. I tried to imagine what things I would miss, but nothing would come to mind. Of course you can only make these observations when you're well off — after all, I knew that after this fire I wouldn't be in need of clothes or a home. Questions of morality can only be asked of the rich: to determine the character of a person you need to ask whether he or she would have had the choice to act differently. Usually a poor person doesn't have that choice. My father would never get over the loss of his Modigliani, that much was for sure. It had been hanging in the drawing room, and had long been 'bitten by the red devil', to use one of the fake Adair's expressions. My mother would shed a few tears because of her designer robes, but on the other hand this was the perfect excuse to disappear for weeks in the luxury boutiques of New York. And as far as Mademoiselle's record collection was concerned . . .

Mademoiselle! At that moment I saw her riding towards the house on the bicycle. Immediately behind her, the first of the fire trucks finally turned into our street. She threw the bicycle onto the pavement and ran up the few steps to the entrance and shouted into the burning building, 'Carlitos!'

'Mademoiselle!' I screamed from the other

side of the street. But she had already disappeared into the house.

'Mademoiselle!' I ran across the street and stood on the pavement. 'Mademoiselle!' The rattling of the fire was so loud that there was no way she could have heard me in there. I ran up the stairs to the front door. 'Mademoiselle!'

The first fireman — I later found out that it was the blond Frank — jumped off the fire truck and grabbed the collar of my jumper. 'Are you crazy? You can't go in there! Do you want to get yourself killed?'

I tore myself free and ran into the house. The staircase was unharmed, but so black that I could hardly recognise it. But I knew the steps and started to run upstairs. I could no longer scream.

* * *

When I came to, I was lying on our neighbour's grass on the opposite side of the street, wrapped in a blanket. Next to me, with an oxygen cylinder and in full fire-fighting uniform, knelt Nick Kowalski, who had obviously been trying to shake me awake for some time. As he was also wearing his helmet it took a while until I recognised him.

'Where is she?' he shouted. And when I

didn't react: 'Tell me where she is! Is she in the house?'

I nodded.

'In the house? Are you sure?'

When I nodded again, he ran across the street. When he ran towards the burning house through the water jet I heard the horrified shouts of his colleagues. 'Nick, are you crazy?', 'Chief, it's no use!', 'Kowalski, get back!'

Up in the house a beam cracked.

I have no recollection of being taken to hospital. When I woke up I found myself in a room with two beds. After many questions the grumpy nurse revealed that I was in the Georgetown University Hospital.

'Is it the high building in the park?'

'That's it.'

'Which floor?'

'Fifth.'

Kindness personified. Of course I first asked her about Mademoiselle, but I couldn't even recollect her name. As much as I thought about it, I just couldn't remember it. That was the shock, the nurse said. What shock? It was a medical term I wouldn't understand at my age. She said that now I should get back to sleep. I wanted to tell her that I would put her forward for the Florence Nightingale award after my recovery. But I was already asleep.

* * *

When I woke up again it was noon, and a few hours later Mademoiselle was wheeled into my room. Infinitely pale, her beautiful hair even shorter than mine as it had apparently caught fire. Her left arm was covered entirely by bandages, but apart from that she didn't seem to have any major injuries. I saw as much when two nurses rolled her off the stretcher and onto the second bed. Like me she was wearing one of the hospital shirts which were open at the back. Luckily her face was unharmed.

She briefly opened her eyes and smiled over to me: 'Carlitos!' Before I could ask her any questions, she had fallen into a deep sleep. Now I could finally remember her name again: Catherine Loucheron.

We had to wait until that evening before we could talk to each other. I had drunk a cup of soup, Mademoiselle wanted nothing. Her good arm was connected by a tube to a transfusion bag, which was hanging on a bar next to her bed. That was more than enough for her, she joked.

As soon as the nurse had left the room, she burst out: 'He saved my life, Carlitos!'

'Who?'

'Who?! Nick Kowalski!'

I was sceptical. 'Is that what he told you?'

'It's even in the papers. First I was on the intensive care ward, I had quite a case of smoke poisoning. One of the doctors read it to me. Nick Kowalski ran into the building, breaking all the rules. He wasn't allowed to, not even as a fireman, as the fire had already reached a certain stage. But he just went inside. He went up to the attic. When he didn't find me there, he went down again. It said in the newspaper that the door to the basement was blocked by a burning beam. But he just pushed it away.'

'You were in the basement? I thought you ran upstairs!'

'That's why you tried to run up the stairs, I know.'

'That was also in the newspapers?'

'Frank went after you and stopped you. He probably told them. Isn't that funny? You went upstairs because you thought that I would look for you there, because I'm so impractical. I went downstairs, because I was sure that with your practical mind, you'd try to shelter in the basement. When I was inside, the beam blocked the door and I couldn't get back out. All the windows were barred! And everything was full of smoke! Apparently he found me under the workbench in your hobby room. He smashed a window and his crew cut open the bars from outside. I must have been with one foot in the grave. In any case, it took him twenty minutes until I was able to breathe properly again.'

'Who?'

'Nick Kowalski, who else? When I came to, he was kneeling next to me and pressing his lips to my mouth.'

'Nick Kowalski?!'

'*Mais oui!* I swear I thought I had died and gone to heaven.'

She tried to laugh but speaking had taken too much out of her. I was already thinking she had fallen asleep when she started to talk again. 'This time you really overdid things, don't you think? When your parents get home they won't even have a bed to sleep in.'

'It was supposed to be a small fire.'

She smiled. 'It was just the right size for me.' And after a while: 'How did he guess that I was inside the house?'

'I told him. I was the only one who saw you run inside. I must have been unconscious when the blond carried me out. But he shook me until I woke up.'

'Who?'

'Nick Kowalski. 'Where is she? Where is she? Is she in the house?' '

'Did you think he cared about me?'

'Cared? He looked like he was scared to death.'

She lifted her head and looked over at me: 'You didn't dream it?'

'One hundred per cent scout's honour.'

I saw her eyes fill with tears. Shortly afterwards she had fallen asleep again.

* * *

The next day was November 21st. Compared with Mademoiselle, who was still sleeping most of the time, I was beginning to feel better by the hour. We had been lying in our room for two days and I began to wonder why no one visited us apart from the doctors and nurses. Apart from the assistant, who had taken care of Mademoiselle on the intensive care ward, no one had sent any flowers. Where were my parents? The flight from Buenos Aires to Washington wouldn't take more than ten hours. Didn't they care what had happened to their daughter? Weren't they interested in the slightest whether their house was still standing?

But the first visitor did come that

afternoon. An unbelievably fat man with an extra wide wedding ring, who introduced himself as the lawyer of the Argentinian embassy. He sat down in the only armchair and wiped the sweat off his forehead with his handkerchief. 'It's not easy to get in here. Of course, I knew that they'd be here. But three policemen to guard a nanny and a child!'

'What policemen?' Mademoiselle asked.

But the lawyer pretended she wasn't there. He returned his handkerchief to his breast pocket and turned to me. 'So you're little Carlota? I of course know your father very well. Greetings first. It took us two days to track down your parents. They were in Patagonia hunting wild boars. They should be on their way back to Washington by now. Tomorrow at the latest, your mummy will be sitting by your side.'

'What policemen, monsieur?' Mademoiselle repeated.

'Well, the ones outside.'

'There are policemen outside?'

'As I said. Three of them.'

'I don't believe you!'

'Nor do I!' I seconded, half-heartedly. I had no trouble believing him.

'That can be helped . . . ' He went to the door, and briefly waved into the corridor. In no time a policeman in full uniform stood in the doorway of our room.

'Thank you,' the lawyer said and closed the door again.

'We're under police protection?' Mademoiselle asked.

'Did I say something about protection?'

'They are guarding us?' she asked, flabbergasted.

'Like two criminals, you mean?' I said it first.

'Didn't you even get the newspapers?' He opened his briefcase and took out a few newspaper clippings, which he didn't hand to Mademoiselle, but to me. For, as a child, I must have been the more innocent of the two. 'You can read them in all peace and quiet. At the moment only let me say this: no confession! You, Carlota, are only allowed to be interrogated in the presence of your parents anyway, understood? And you, miss, are still down as unfit to give evidence. I arranged that with the doctors, and that's what the press will hear again today. When Carlota's parents are back, we'll see.' He nodded in the direction of both our beds and left.

* * *

The next hour we spent reading the press, and unfortunately it wasn't only the local one. The *New York Post* had dedicated a whole page to us, with photographs of Mademoiselle, but also of Nick Kowalski and the New Age Luisita. A series of mysterious arson attacks in Georgetown, Washington's most exclusive district, was close to being solved. A certain Catherine Loucheron, governess with a high-ranking Argentinian diplomat's family, was the prime suspect, who apparently in cahoots with the daughter of the house set a series of fires which had caused damage in the region of ten million dollars. The crucial information came from the fiancée of the local fire chief, a hairdresser who accused him of being their accomplice. While the governess and child, who had fallen victim to their own arson attack, were recuperating under strict police guard at Georgetown University Hospital, the chief of the fire department, Nick Kowalski, had vanished without a trace. It wouldn't be the first time that a member of the fire department had been involved in a case of pyromania. One would have to wait until the governess, a French woman of spectacular beauty, could be interrogated.

Mademoiselle was the first to react. 'So we're in a trap.'

'Looks like it.'

'Carlitos, you're innocent, understood? You know and knew nothing!'

'I'm a child and they can't do much to me. The child of a diplomat! You knew nothing!'

Mademoiselle sat up in her bed and looked towards the window. 'How high up are we? Maybe we can get out through the window?'

'Fifth floor.'

She let herself sink back into her pillow. 'Too high.'

* * *

But it wasn't too high. At least not for someone like Nick Kowalski. This part will be the most difficult to tell, I know, because it is the most difficult to believe. But I swear that this is the way it happened: it was a happy ending like in the movies. One of the old movies, because these days no scriptwriter would dare to invent such a happy ending.

I don't know how late it was, but in any case it was pitch dark. If the emergency light hadn't been on in our room — it's lit so the nurse doesn't have to turn on the lights when she attends to a patient — you wouldn't have been able to see your own hand. Mademoiselle was standing bathed in this blue light and called my name quietly.

'Carlitos . . . Carlitos, wake up! I want to say goodbye!'

'Goodbye?' She had woken me from deepest sleep.

'Yes, I have to go.' She stood there looking like a statue, which apart from the unreal lighting, must have also been due to the fact that she had draped one of the white sheets over her short night-gown.

'But that's impossible! The police are outside the door!'

'I'm not going through the door.' She turned and pointed towards the window.

When I sat up in bed and looked at the window, I, at least for a split second, seemed to lose all sense of reality. In any case, it was the first and last time that I seriously believed in the possibilities of apparitions. On the other side of the open window I could see Nick Kowalski, from the waist upward. He waved at me, smiling. 'Hi, young lady,' he said quietly. 'Sorry to wake you.'

I must have looked so flabbergasted that Mademoiselle had to laugh. 'He's not floating out there,' she whispered. 'He is standing on the fire ladder.'

She sat down on my bed. 'Carlitos, we don't have much time and I have to say adieu.' She took me in her arms and hugged me tightly. 'Perhaps we won't see each other again. Perhaps we don't even want to see each other again, for whatever else we could experience together would be banal. But I want you to know one thing: I will never, never, never forget you!' When she let go of me, I saw that her eyes were full of tears. 'Charlotte, *mon amour. Je te dois tout mon bonheur!*'

She planted a thick kiss on my forehead, walked over to the window, climbed up onto the sill, from which Kowalski helped her to the other side. Now I leapt out of bed and walked the few steps towards the window. There they stood like a framed wedding couple: she all in white, he in his fireman's uniform. The feeling that I must have been dreaming simply didn't go away.

'Good luck, young lady,' Kowalski grinned. 'And no more fires, OK? What was it this time?'

'Paint thinner.'

He laughed quietly. 'Not bad.'

They had already climbed down two rungs — only their heads were still visible in the window — when I finally remembered to ask, 'Where're you going?'

Mademoiselle looked at Kowalski with a smile. 'No idea. I didn't ask.'

She threw me a kiss and then they continued with the descent. I stayed at the window and looked after them. The ladder was part of the fire truck he had shown me on my visit to the fire station. It was extended to its maximum length — if we had been a floor higher it just wouldn't have been long enough. They climbed down as quickly as they could. Kowalski was two steps below Mademoiselle, so he could catch her in an emergency. But Mademoiselle climbed as agilely as if she had never done anything else in her life but climb fire ladders. At first she looked up at me again and again and I waved down to her. But soon it was too dark to make out her face. If she hadn't been wearing the white sheet, I wouldn't even have known when they had reached the bottom.

And then Kowalski began to retract the ladder and a moment later I heard him start the engine. He drove in darkness to the street with his spectacular catch, and only then he switched on the headlights and immediately afterwards the siren. It sounded like a siren of triumph, and I was almost sure that he had turned it on only for me. In any case it wasn't very cautious.

✾

What else is there to report? In normal circumstances, this would all have become quite a scandal: a fireman who misuses his office to kidnap a French woman suspected of multiple arson from the hospital. But the whole thing didn't even make the papers. The day after that was November 22nd 1963, and at 12.30 p.m. the shots in Dallas were fired. Everyone can imagine the mayhem that caused in Washington. For weeks — no, months — there was no other subject than the murder of John F. Kennedy.

As for me, I was handed over to a psychiatrist as soon as I was released from hospital. I had to see her three times a week for a chat. But the psychiatrist has yet to be born who gets something out of me that I don't want to say. Mrs Engel was a Jew from Germany, and, as a thirteen-year-old — I too had in the meantime turned thirteen — had had to flee the Gestapo under amazing circumstances. I would have been deadly ashamed to tell such a woman about my little problems with Mummy and Daddy. I know that most people who go to an analyst couldn't care less. For them it is a highly paid garbage removal service for the rubbish which they have amassed in their heads, which, most of the time, they regard as highly interesting food for thought, and an obstacle only when they embark on the highly interesting journey to 'discover themselves'.

My God, as if there was something to be found with people like that! I still don't know today quite how I managed it, but by the third session we were discussing exclusively Mrs Engel's horrific childhood.

As far as the fires were concerned, the last one was put down to the negligence of the diplomat's daughter who was smoking in her hideaway. The other fires weren't even mentioned and the report against Mademoiselle was dismissed as the malicious hearsay of a deserted lover. A governess who risked her life to save the child in her care couldn't possibly be a criminal.

⋆ ⋆ ⋆

But Mademoiselle had disappeared, and no one ever heard from her or Nick Kowalski again. When I rang his private number after a year or so, the fake Adair was on the phone, not the New Age Luisita. Yes, he now lived in his house and was also taking care of the pigeons. Luisita had moved to California soon after Kowalski's disappearance, from where she occasionally sent postcards. She had married a brother in faith, and was running a practice for taking people back.

'Taking back where?'

'To a former life,' the fake Adair replied,

emotionless. No, unfortunately he knew as much of Kowalski as I did. No one had ever heard from him again. Did I want to go and see a football match with him?

I bought a postcard, with a picture of a pair of pigeons, put it in an envelope and sent it without return address to Mademoiselle's parents in Biarritz. On the postcard I wrote in printed letters that they could fly back as the cat had lost its bite — meaning the New Age Luisita as well as the US Justice Department. I didn't want to risk more. I never got a reply.

* * *

Six months later my father was once again transferred. Not as hoped to Paris, but to Stockholm, of course as ambassador — but my French lessons had therefore been in vain. My parents finally got a divorce in Stockholm, as my father had immediately embarked on an affair with a very young Swedish woman. First I moved with my mother to Vienna and then to London. Oddly enough, there I developed a real interest in the violin, which after all I had only taken up to avoid Mr Pilgrim's piano lessons. In short, I became a violinist. As, after a few setbacks, I was finally accepted into the London Philharmonic Orchestra, I had to travel even more than I used to during my childhood as a diplomat's daughter. On one occasion, after a concert at the New York Lincoln Center, there was a reception attended by Caroline Kennedy. She was now an attractive young woman and, compared to the first occasion I met her, she even seemed to enjoy her official role. Or maybe she had even been touched by our music? We conversed for a while, but I didn't mention that we had almost played together as children.

* * *

I thought of Mademoiselle almost every day. When I sometimes managed not to think of her, I met her in one of my dreams. These were usually incomprehensible or banal, but never frightening. Once, for example, we were walking on a pier out into the sea. When we arrived at the end she gave me two of her super-light kisses.

'Why only two?' I complained.

'There were always only two,' she smiled.

As we were talking about numbers, I reminded her that she had only told me one of her father's six rules.

'Which one?' she asked and smiled.

'The man always has to take the first step.'

'Only the number changes with the others.

Rule number two: the man always has to take the second step. Rule number three: the man always has to take the third step . . . and so on. The woman can only take the seventh step. But only a small one, otherwise he'll be scared.'

'But it was different with Nick Kowalski?'

She looked at me, one of her eyes pebble-grey, the other almost black. 'But Nick Kowalski is a real man.'

* * *

I know I should have simply gone to Biarritz and interrogated her family, but I was too afraid to find out something negative: the two must have been happy! On a tour through Canada I once consulted a Tarot reader. Of course I gave her too much money and as precise dates as I could, as I only wanted to hear good and believable news: a beautiful French girl and a fireman disappeared from America one night — she should tell me what happened to them. She arranged her twenty-two cards into a circle and pointed at three which lay together: a curly-haired blonde woman sitting under the stars, a man at the foot of a broken tower and a nude couple holding hands in the fat sun. Good news, she said: both were in Paris where the man had once again found a job with the fire department and they were completely happy. Even though I of course didn't believe a word she said, I was so reassured that my thoughts of Mademoiselle became less frequent. And that's why I now occasionally tell myself that you should evaluate a belief not according to its truth content but according to its usefulness. But it's precisely this that believers don't seem to want.

The Tarot reader wanted to tell me about my own love life, but after all, I knew that myself. Of course I had also succumbed to the temptation of marriage: I had married, had divorced, married again, divorced again. There followed a series of more or less exciting affairs, with a peculiarity which I only discovered later: like Mademoiselle at the football ground I also wanted to be the one who said 'I love you' first, as if I could conjure up the passion which she had experienced for Nick Kowalski. And all the love letters I wrote! Funny ones, sentimental ones, poetic ones, sarcastic ones, erotic ones — sometimes on the same day with the same words to different men. Maybe I thought my hidden talents for an all-enveloping love would be most likely to come to fruition if I sowed the seed as wide as possible.

Occasionally I also cast myself in the role

of the sufferer: 'I had hoped that maybe one day you'd love me after all,' I wrote to someone who I knew could never love me as he was playing the same charade as my Argentinian uncle. And of course apart from these banal stories, there were important affairs during which I didn't write any love letters. But when I was lying in the arms of one of these men, even in the moment of deepest passion, I always told myself: that's not how it was with Mademoiselle.

Then *you* came. One frosty January night, after a concert, in this, your town. I simply stayed and started to light all these fires, to conquer you.

Other titles published by The House of Ulverscroft:

THE VALLEY OF THE VINES

Mark Neilson

Sophie Hargreaves hopes to repair her shattered family by buying a rundown vineyard in Piedmont and bringing everyone together again. Sadly, her attempt fails and she's left struggling to bring in the grape harvest on her own before she faces ruin. Then, just as she begins to lose hope, Sophie finds help from an unlikely source: three strangers fleeing a storm and its flooding. They find themselves wrestling with the problems of saving the grapes and making the ancient winery viable. Unexpectedly, Sophie finds a new life in the remote wine valleys of Northern Italy.

FAR ABOVE RUBIES

Anne-Marie Vukelic

Married to one of the most famous novelists of the Victorian era, the life of Catherine Dickens is as absorbing as any of Charles Dickens' novels. Set against the backdrop of London in the nineteenth century, Catherine recounts the story of her marriage to a restless, mercurial husband. Well known Victorians William Thackeray, Wilkie Collins and the colourful Count D'Orsay live once more through the pages of Catherine's intriguing novel. Many fascinating people lie in tombs above which 'no Trophies are raised'. Catherine Dickens may be one to whom this applies, but here she speaks for herself . . .

PLAYING FOR KEEPS

Sally Wragg

Generations of the Vernon family have been involved with Rislington Rovers Football Club, otherwise known as the Rogues. But now the Rogues are not only faced with relegation but also an ongoing investigation into the club's financial affairs. The mayhem within the club is matched only by the turmoil of Vernon family life. Eleanor Vernon, wife of Rogues stalwart Landon, hates the influence the game has on her family, but things are about to get much worse. The Rogues are seeking a new chief executive and the shock appointment threatens the very core of Vernon family life . . .

MS. HEMPEL CHRONICLES

Sarah Shun-Lien Bynum

Ms. Beatrice Hempel has just taken her first job as an English teacher. Closer in age and sensibility to her pupils than to her colleagues, she spends her time outside of school hours reading, writing, listening to rock and roll, and wondering whether she really was right to get engaged. In the classroom, too, she feels 'in-between'. Still young enough to understand her students' way of seeing things, she wants to be their accomplice; but she also feels a terrible responsibility as the adult witness to their adolescent growing pains.

THE LONGSHOT

Katie Kitamura

Cal and his long-standing friend and trainer Riley are on their way to Mexico for a make-or-break rematch with the legendary Rivera, who has never been beaten. Four years ago, Cal became the only fighter to ever take Rivera the distance, even though it nearly ended him. Only Riley, who has been at his side for the last ten years, knows how much that fight changed everything for Cal. And only Riley really knows what's now at stake, for both of them . . .

SPECIAL MESSAGE TO READERS

This book is published under the auspices of

THE ULVERSCROFT FOUNDATION

(registered charity No. 264873 UK)

Established in 1972 to provide funds for research, diagnosis and treatment of eye diseases. Examples of contributions made are: —

A Children's Assessment Unit at Moorfield's Hospital, London.

•

Twin operating theatres at the Western Ophthalmic Hospital, London.

•

A Chair of Ophthalmology at the Royal Australian College of Ophthalmologists.

•

The Ulverscroft Children's Eye Unit at the Great Ormond Street Hospital For Sick Children, London.

You can help further the work of the Foundation by making a donation or leaving a legacy. Every contribution, no matter how small, is received with gratitude. Please write for details to:

THE ULVERSCROFT FOUNDATION,
The Green, Bradgate Road, Anstey,
Leicester LE7 7FU, England.
Telephone: (0116) 236 4325

In Australia write to:

THE ULVERSCROFT FOUNDATION,
c/o The Royal Australian and New Zealand
College of Ophthalmologists,
94-98 Chalmers Street, Surry Hills,
N.S.W. 2010, Australia

Esther Vilar is a Buenos Aires-born playwright. Her numerous plays include *The American Popess*, *Speer* and *Jealousy*.